'I can play emperor,' Conor said softly, 'crack the whip, demand anything...indulge all my whims.' His eyes rested on Diana's mouth. 'You're one of my whims, Diana. And you're unfortunate enough to find yourself in my power. And for the duration of this film...' his eyes scrutinised her angry face '...I want to see you play Cleopatra to my Caesar!'

'You can't force me to do anything!' she said with fierce determination not to give in. 'Not a thing!'

'No,' he agreed coolly, 'but I can make life damned near unliveable if you refuse to indulge me.'

FORBIDDEN PASSION

BY

SARAH HOLLAND

MILLS & BOON LIMITED
ETON HOUSE   18-24 PARADISE ROAD
RICHMOND   SURREY   TW9 1SR

*First published in Great Britain 1991
by Mills & Boon Limited*

© Sarah Holland 1991

*Australian copyright 1991
Philippine copyright 1991
This edition 1991*

ISBN 0 263 77236 5

*Set in Times Roman 10 on 10¼ pt.
01-9109-64225 C*

Made and printed in Great Britain

CHAPTER ONE

DIANA was getting dressed when the call came.

Like a bird in a gilded cage, she stood in the gilt-edged suite at the Ritz, zipping up her pink silk suit, her long hair cascading like golden silk down her slender back. Birthday cards stood on the marble mantelpiece. Gifts were strewn on the pink silk coverlet of her vast double bed.

She was twenty-four today, and nothing felt as she had expected it to. She didn't feel older, she didn't feel wiser; she felt exactly as she had yesterday, and the day before...

Sun shone through the french windows, and outside London glittered in the July heatwave, traffic streaming down Piccadilly, red buses and black taxis and limousines all nudging one another from Park Lane to Fortnum's.

It was almost midday. Diana studied herself in the mirror, biting her lip. The pink silk emphasised her full breasts, nipped in at the waist and flared out in a peplum above her slender hips.

The clock began to chime the hour.

The telephone shrilled into life.

Diana hesitated, then walked across the deep-pile pink carpet to answer it.

'Hello?'

The line crackled.

Diana frowned. 'Hello? Diana Sullivan speaking.'

There was another pause.

'Hello, Diana...' said a dark male voice, and her heart stopped beating as the years slipped away and she felt the shock slam into her mind like a roller-coaster speeding to destruction.

Heart thudding, mouth dry, she whispered, 'Who is this?'

He gave a soft, mocking laugh. 'Don't tell me you've forgotten, Diana! Not on your birthday!'

'Who is this?' she demanded hoarsely, beginning to tremble.

'Say my name!' the voice commanded. 'Say it!'

Her hand was damp on the receiver, her whole body quivering. 'Conor...?'

'You remembered,' he said under his breath, dark threat steel-lining his voice. 'And so did I, Diana!'

'How did you know I was here?' she whispered fiercely, heart thudding. 'Are you in the country? Are you in London?'

'I'm very close,' he said softly. 'I can even see you. Standing at the window...wearing pink...you were always so pretty in pink...'

'Oh, my God!' Diana caught her breath, jerking back instinctively from the long, wide french windows of her suite. 'Conor! My God, have you lost your mind? Don't you realise what——?'

'Happy anniversary,' he cut in bitingly, 'my love!'

The line went dead.

For a few seconds she just stood there, clutching the receiver in damp fingers, staring blankly at the birthday cards on the mantelpiece and listening to that sinister, endless, black dialling tone.

Conor!

Shaking, she replaced the receiver, sinking down slowly on to the chair beside her and struggling to breathe steadily. He couldn't be here! He couldn't be in London...not today, not today of all days, six years after it had all happened. Six years to the day...oh, God, and watching her from another window: watching her dress, watching the pink silk suit slide on over her pink silk lingerie. She shuddered convulsively, her whole body throbbing with awareness, awareness of those eyes, those passionate, hot blue eyes watching her broodingly from a secret window opposite the Ritz on Piccadilly...

Eleanor's bedroom door slammed shut. Her footsteps approached Diana's room.

Diana jumped to her feet, heart pounding, struggling to look calm as the door opened and her guardian Eleanor Sullivan walked into the bedroom.

'Who was that?' Eleanor was elegant as always, but so cold, her head held erect and her red mouth tight.

'Just the hotel management, ringing to wish me happy birthday.' Diana picked up her pink handbag, desperate to run from the room as though by running from the telephone she would run from Conor Slade. 'Shall we go? We're supposed to be there at twelve-thirty...'

'Well, I'm ready,' Eleanor said, following Diana to the door. 'It's just you who leaves everything to the last minute.'

Diana compressed her lips. That call from Conor had shaken her to her roots and she needed time to think—not fence with her guardian.

'Frankly,' said Eleanor, 'I think it's quite absurd of them to replace the director of your new film at such short notice.'

'Yes.' Diana walked down the hall of the suite and opened the front door. 'I was so looking forward to working with Teddy Godwin!'

'And I was looking forward to meeting him.'

'He's a great director.' Diana spoke as though in another world, her mind whirling with thoughts of Conor, of that telephone call, of the sound of his dark, dangerous voice.

Eleanor stepped out into the deep-pink corridor. 'Godwin is a marvel of a man! Such an artist! Such a genius!'

'Yes...' Diana wondered if Conor would try to approach her again, and her whole body throbbed with alarm as she walked down the corridor to the lift. Was Conor still out there, still watching the Ritz? Would he see her walk out, follow her even? He was capable of anything! A trained killer, an ex-SAS man—what was he doing in London?

· Diana fought to stay calm and pressed the call button of the lift.

'I don't know who the replacement is,' said Eleanor, 'but I have no doubt he's not a patch on Godwin. Otherwise why would they summon us to this mysterious luncheon?'

'Georgina said she wanted us to meet him personally before filming started,' Diana said, and suddenly thought: Conor went into films three years ago. Conor went into films...oh, God...She leant weakly against the wall by the lift. It couldn't be Conor! He was a director now, filming battle scenes and gunfights.

'But why not simply tell us who he is?' Eleanor stepped into the lift, reflected in the mirrored walls. She was a tall woman, matchlessly elegant in an austere black dress, a three-stranded rope of pearls at her throat and pearl studs in her ears. Her black hair was swept into its customary chignon, and her pillarbox-red lipstick echoed a bygone age.

'Georgina said it was because she wanted to surprise us.' Diana suddenly realised what could happen today: but no, she couldn't think of it! Mustn't think of what would happen if Conor Slade ever got her in his power.

'Georgina Coral is a nuisance,' Eleanor said tightly as the lift doors slid shut. 'I realise she's director of Coral Films, but she's also a thoroughly *risqué* Merry Widow and the last word in vulgarity. You know I loathe her.'

'I know, Eleanor.' Diana pressed for the ground floor. 'But she's an important and influential lady, and in this case she holds all the cards. It's her family's company, her film, and her choice of director.'

'In other words, it's a *fait accompli*.'

'It does seem that way.'

'But why all the secrecy?'

'Your guess is as good as mine.' Diana refused to consider the possibility of Conor's being appointed. It was too remote. 'But she told me this morning that the new director was an exciting choice.'

'How typical of Georgina!' Eleanor sniffed. 'I'm surprised she didn't say he was "divinely thrilling"!'

Diana laughed, eyes sparkling. She did adore Georgina.

The lift doors slid open.

The Palm Court was busy, impeccably dressed guests sipping champagne and talking between the tall pink marble pillars, the lush green palms and the bronze statues of the gods.

'If the director's a wash-out,' said Eleanor as they walked to the swing door, 'you'll have to cancel the film. I'll tell them myself if——'

'You will not, Eleanor, tell them anything,' Diana said firmly. 'We begin filming in three days' time. I can't possibly back out at this stage. It would be unprofessional and unfair.' They swept out through the revolving door, stepping on to Piccadilly, and the liveried doorman came rushing up to them with a salute.

'A taxi, my man!' Eleanor said with an imperious lift of her head.

The man ran out into the middle of the road, to be almost knocked over by a large glittering red bus that chugged past in the hot July air. A black taxi screeched to a halt, and Diana walked towards it, aware of the stares of passers-by who had recognised her and were whispering, 'Isn't that Diana Sullivan...?'

'Soho Square!' Eleanor rapped out to the driver as the door shut.

The wheels spun. Sun flashed off Green Park as they drove away into the traffic, and Diana looked out of the windows thinking, Is he in London? Is he here? How did he know I was at the Ritz? There was no publicity...

She could see him so clearly in her mind's eye. Even now, even after six years she could see him...that livid scar on his cheekbone, the blue eyes that blazed above it and the tough, sensual mouth below.

It was their anniversary, and she admitted as she stared out at Marble Arch in the July sunlight that she had known it as she had awoken this morning...known it

as her twenty-fourth birthday had approached...
known it and hoped to hear from him.

Every birthday she thought of Conor. Every day she
struggled to keep him from her mind, but on birthdays—
every birthday since her eighteenth—she had woken to
the memory of Conor, the memory of Conor Slade, of
dark passion and the penalties paid for having experienced it.

Into her mind flashed the black mountains of
Connemara, the red-gold sun blazing down on two lovers
entwined in passion and despair, their fierce moans of
pleasure echoing that bloodstained Celtic sky...

'Soho Square!' announced the taxi driver, and Diana's
head snapped up, eyes startled as she dragged herself
from that vivid moment in time. She got out of the taxi,
the summer sunshine lighting up her hair.

The smoked-glass doors of Coral Films swung open
as the doorman bowed to them. They swept in, Diana
smiling at the receptionist, who grinned at her and waved.

They rode up in the private lift, and the chairman's
secretary showed them to the boardroom. The wide oak-
panelled fifteenth-floor penthouse overlooked the whole
of London through panoramic windows, and the long
oak table was set for four people.

'Darlings!' Georgina Coral sailed towards them, magnificent in a purple dress that emphasised her voluptuous bosom and vivacious smile, and enfolded Diana in
a scented embrace. 'Marvellous to see you, Diana!
Happy birthday...you look absolutely wonderful!'

Diana smiled, and kissed her. 'Hello, Georgina! You
look lovely, too.' Georgina always looked marvellous.

'And Eleanor!' Georgina turned, bestowing a cool
smile on Eleanor but not kissing her. Nobody ever dared
kiss Eleanor. 'Impeccable as ever! May I offer you a
drink? Diana?'

'Thank you.' Diana inclined her blonde head.

'Champagne?' Georgina suggested with a smile.

'What a lovely idea!' Diana laughed.

'I don't approve of drinking at luncheon,' said Eleanor
icily.

'Well,' Georgina poured a glass of Dom Perignon, 'this is something of a celebration, Eleanor, isn't it? After all—it is her birthday.'

'Yes...' Diana murmured, accepting the glass, and remembering Conor...somehow the two words had become inextricably linked. Birthday and Conor, Conor and birthday. Would she ever forget?

'And I, for one,' said Georgina with a bright smile, 'can't wait for tonight!'

'It's so kind of you to throw a birthday party for me, Georgina!' Diana said at once. 'I can't tell you how much I'm looking forward to it.'

'Well, my dear!' Georgina flashed vivacious green eyes. 'It's such a marvellous excuse to throw a bash!'

Diana laughed, and drank a little champagne.

'And I've invited absolutely everyone, darling,' Georgina went on. 'I'm sure I'll have even more fun than you!'

'Hmm,' Eleanor said, eyes narrowing. 'Now, look here, Georgina, I want to know what on earth is going on. Why all the secrecy about this new director? And why did you replace Godwin at the last minute?'

'Godwin backed out.' Georgina poured herself some champagne. 'There was nothing any of us could do. We had to get someone on short notice, and we were lucky enough to get Conor Slade.'

The champagne glass fell from Diana's fingers.

'Oh!' she cried on a hoarse whisper, jerking back as glass shattered around her and icy champagne splattered her slender legs, a shard of glass embedding itself in her ankle.

'Diana!' Georgina leapt to her aid, removing the glass from her ankle.

'Oh, God!' Diana whispered, staring at the smidgeon of blood, and remembering that other day, that other shower of tiny fragments of glass all around them as Conor Slade had lain on top of her and shielded her face with his strong dark-haired hands.

'Diana!' Eleanor spat, eyes furious. 'Pull yourself together!'

'I didn't know!' she said hoarsely, staring at Eleanor in a sudden moment of icy panic. 'I swear I didn't know!'

'It's not a serious cut——' Georgina was straightening, the tiny shard of glass in her hand '—but I'll ring down for some—— '

The intercom buzzed loudly.

All three turned to stare at it.

Then Georgina turned, pressed the intercom and said lightly, 'Yes? What is it?'

'Mr Slade's on his way up, Mrs Coral,' crackled the receptionist's voice.

Diana moaned aloud, stumbling back from Eleanor, her hands at her face as she felt the panic close in on her, gripping her mind with icy fingers, telling her she would never survive...

'Diana,' Georgina said slowly, 'I can see you're very upset, but I really must ask you to remember you're a professional actress, and you must accept my choice of director.'

'But Conor Slade...' Diana began hoarsely.

Suddenly there were footsteps in the outer office, the door-handle was turning, and she gasped, looking over at the door with wide panic-stricken blue eyes.

The door was flung open and Conor Slade strode in.

Her heart stopped beating as she saw him.

He was more sexy, more masculine, more dangerous than ever. The fierce blue eyes blazed above a strong nose and a tough, uncompromising mouth. His face was tanned, his bone-structure like the rocks of Connemara, hewn in jagged lines and flaring with passion at his mouth.

He was six feet four of raw power, his broad shoulders encased in a magnificent black business suit, a gold watch-chain glittering across his powerful chest, his long legs muscled and his black shoes polished to a high gloss.

But the civilised clothes of twentieth-century masculine authority did not hide the memory of her fierce, passionate, obsessive Celtic lover, and the scar on his tough cheekbone made him look like a warrior king.

'Mr Slade!' Georgina trilled, walking to him brightly. 'Marvellous to see you, darling.'

'Georgina...' Conor had to bend his dark head: he always towered over people. Georgina's red lips pressed against his cheek and Diana's mouth went dry as she remembered the taste and feel of his skin.

Georgina took his arm. 'Allow me to formally introduce you to your leading lady, Miss Diana——'

'We've met,' Conor Slade drawled. 'I wonder if the lady remembers...?'

'Yes...' Diana said tightly. 'I remember!' And inside, the whirlpool of forbidden desire began again.

Conor moved slowly towards her, and she had to force herself not to back off. He stopped, towering over her, his dark head obliterating the light. The blue eyes travelled with insolent assessment over her body, lingering on her full breasts, slender waist and sensually curved hips.

'My dear,' he said softly, raising his gaze to hers, 'you're more ravishing than ever.'

Diana stared at him, her eyes blazing, fighting the sex appeal that radiated out of him, fighting the burning response that leapt inside her so shamefully, wantonly, her eyes staring at every inch of him even as she struggled not to look.

'And what a charming outfit,' Conor said softly, eyes returning to her breasts beneath the pink silk. 'Why... I almost feel I've seen it before!'

She was breathless, her heart racing violently at the thought of his seeing her dress from that window high above Piccadilly, seeing her move innocently in brief pink lingerie while the fantasies of revenge moved through his dark, dangerous mind.

'Isn't it a special day today?' Conor was laughing at her, his blue eyes satanic. 'Georgina mentioned something about a celebration. A personal celebration, of course. Nothing to do with the film... with my appointment as director...'

'No,' Diana whispered thickly. 'No, there's no celebration.'

'An anniversary, perhaps?' Conor drawled, eyes mocking her.

She went white, passionate hatred blazing in her eyes—would he mention it? Say it out loud? Did he have no sense of decency whatsoever?

'It's her birthday!' Georgina's words saved her as she appeared with a glass of champagne, her green eyes anxious. 'She is twenty-four today!'

'Ah!' Conor took his glass, towering over Diana, his mouth hardening. 'Your birthday. Twenty-four...and you look so very young. Tell me, Miss Sullivan—have you ever been married?'

Diana went rigid.

'Twenty-four can be very young indeed!' Eleanor's voice cut in sharply. 'I always say a girl is not a woman until she is thirty!'

Conor's blue eyes flicked like razors to Eleanor. 'You think so?'

'I know so!' Eleanor lifted her head. 'I brought her up—remember?'

'And seem extremely reluctant to relinquish your role as guardian,' Conor said under his breath, blue eyes ruthless.

Eleanor glared at him, rigid with dislike.

'I do so love birthdays!' trilled Georgina, handing Diana another glass. 'They're such a perfect excuse for champagne!' She raised her own glass in a toast. 'And it's such wonderfully sinful stuff!'

'I've always thought birthdays were an excellent excuse,' Conor drawled, 'for all kinds of sin.'

Diana's mouth was dry as she took her champagne, heart thudding erratically. 'We should be celebrating the start of the film—surely!'

'On this day?' Conor said tightly. 'I think not.'

'But it's the real reason we're all here together!'

'Want to put that to the vote?'

She said thickly, 'Conor, please...'

'A toast!' Conor said in a hard, menacing voice. 'A toast to you, my love. To your twenty-fourth birthday and all it brings you!'

Diana looked up into those passionate blue eyes and felt rocked by his impact. 'I don't want to drink a toast to——'

'To all the pleasure of being twenty-four,' he said under his breath, eyes intent on her face, 'and all the pain.'

She shivered. How could he be so blatant? So cruel?

'To the rewards,' he said softly, clinking his glass against hers, 'and the punishments!'

Diana was breathless, hating him, wanting him, hating herself. He was her nemesis, and, now that they were face to face again, all she could do was stare at him, see the dangerous good looks and the passion in his blue eyes and the strong, muscular body beneath that civilised and impeccable suit...she was burning up with conflict!

'I won't drink to that!' Eleanor's voice said cuttingly. 'I won't drink to it and I won't allow this charade to continue for another——'

'Let's drink to the film, then!' Georgina said quickly, raising her glass. 'A toast to *The Virgin and The Unicorn*! To its star, Diana Sullivan, and its director—Conor Slade!'

There was a brief, tense silence, then they all drank their champagne; but it tasted like ashes in Diana's mouth and she wondered if she would even be able to stand much longer, because being near Conor again had turned her whole body into a throbbing minefield of awareness and she didn't know whether she wanted him to walk out and never come back, or grab her, pin her against the wall and kiss her until she moaned helplessly against that hard, passionate mouth...

'I've got to do something!' Diana said hoarsely as she walked back into her suite at the Ritz two hours later. 'I can't just sit back and let this happen!'

Eleanor followed her, closing the door. 'You must take immediate action.'

'But what can I do?' Diana went into the living-room, threw her bag on to the couch. 'The contract's signed, I can't get out of it!'

'You could see your agent,' Eleanor suggested.

'Of course!' Diana turned. 'I'll go there straight away! He's only a taxi ride away, and——' She stopped, heart sinking. 'How can I? I'll be seen going into his office! Georgina will know I'm trying to welch on the deal and——'

'I could go,' said Eleanor, eyes intent. 'No one would notice me.'

Hope lit Diana's eyes. 'Yes! That's it! You go—tell him I'll do anything to get out of the contract. Anything at all. Tell him——'

Eleanor was already walking to the door. 'Don't you worry, Diana! I'll make sure he gets you out of this!'

Diana ran after her. 'And come straight back to tell me what he says!'

The door slammed. Diana sighed, ran a hand through her blonde hair and walked back into the silent living-room. Would she get out of the contract?

She rang room service, ordered some tea, then sat on the couch, forcing herself to relax. But how could she relax, knowing Conor had her in his power again?

Eventually, the doorbell rang. Diana went to answer it, expecting room service with her tea as she opened the door, and her mouth was curved in a charming smile as she looked up into blue, blazing eyes.

'My love!' Conor bit out, blue eyes blazing.

Diana gasped and tried to slam the door.

He pushed it with the flat of his hand and as it smashed back on its hinges Diana was backing off, her slim hands up to protect herself from his powerful body.

'Don't back away from me, my love!' Conor drawled softly, shutting the door. 'It makes me want to punish you for what you've done to me...'

'Don't!' she said fiercely, shaking, backing. 'Don't come any closer!'

'But I want to!' he said under his breath, backing her against the wall, towering over her, obliterating the light with his dark head. 'I want to punish you for what you've put me through...for the last six years...six years without love, without light, without——'

'Nobody said you had to live without those things!' she burst out hoarsely, staring up at him, a pulse throbbing wildly in her throat. 'All I did was make sure you couldn't come near me!'

'Why couldn't I come near you, Diana?' he demanded. 'We were lovers!'

'Enemies!'

'Lovers!' he bit out. 'And more! My God, we were so much in love that we couldn't keep our hands off each other!'

'No!' she denied fiercely. 'That's a dirty lie! I hated you!'

'Oh, no, Diana,' he said softly, blue eyes gleaming with cat-like malice as he smiled, pressing her against the wall and enjoying his power as he deliberately ran a hand through her long blonde hair. 'Hated me? Hated? You used to go up in flames at the touch of my hand!'

'It's not true!' she whispered, shaking, eyes blazing. 'Not true!'

'Don't you remember our first date?' he drawled under his breath, his hard thighs brushing hers as he moved closer. 'How you stared at my mouth all night, how you jumped when I touched your hand...?'

'I don't remember anything like that!'

'And how you started to moan as soon as I kissed you?' he said thickly. 'Started to moan and clutch my shoulders and shake...? Oh, yes, just as I did, Diana, just as I did!' His hand tightened in her hair. 'I shook too, Diana! Remember that! Remember how I pushed you back in the front of the car and almost fell on you?'

'I was nothing more than a child!' she flung, heart thudding. 'I was naïve!'

'You were dynamite,' he said tightly, eyes hating her, 'and you exploded like a firebomb when I finally got you into my bed!'

'I hated you!' she said again, breathing erratically. 'Do you hear me? *Hated* you!'

'Oh, you hated me so much you ran away with me to Ireland and married me!' he said tightly. 'And now you turn white at the sight of me and——'

'You're hurting me!' she cried, desperate to stop him
before he mentioned Connemara. 'Let go!' She tried to
jerk away from him, but smashed into the hall table,
knocking it to the floor with a thud and a crash as the
vase of flowers fell off it and water streamed into the
carpet with the red rose petals falling in it like drops of
blood.

There was a long silence. They stared at one another
in that silent, civilised hallway, and both were breathing
hard as their eyes met and Diana knew she would never
get out of this without speaking the truth, without saying
what he had come here to force out of her.

'We were divorced,' she whispered, trembling, struggling to find the courage to face him as an equal, suddenly very beautiful and very young. 'You know we were
divorced! The decree absolute came through in——'

'Summer three years ago,' he said under his breath,
and thrust his hands into the black trouser pockets of
his impeccable suit, his mouth hard and his blue eyes
fixed intently on her face.

Diana breathed unevenly. 'Then if you received the
decree absolute, surely you can see how impossible
this——?'

'Do you have any idea what it did to me to see it in
black and white?' he asked tightly, his voice low but
strained. 'To know how completely you had cut me off?
Cut me out of your life?'

'I . . .' she moistened her lips, and his narrowed eyes
followed the little movement ' . . . I had to!'

'Don't tell me you had to! And don't tell me that injunction was necessary either!'

'It . . . it was . . .'

'We were man and wife!' he bit out, eyes blazing. 'We
could have talked about it. Worked it through, whatever
the problem was.'

'It . . . it was too much!' she said huskily. 'I didn't know
what to say, how to tell you . . .'

'Liar!' he said thickly, eyes hating her. 'You just ran
from the confrontation, as you run from every damned
confrontation, and hoped you'd get away with it as you

always have before!' He stepped forwards, his body bristling with aggression as he towered over her. 'Well, you're not running any more, Diana! This is where the running stops! Once and for all! Even if I have to break you up into tiny pieces and fling you screaming into the void, I'll make you face me!'

'I am facing you!' she said with stung pride.

'You're backing away from me with every move I make towards you!' he said angrily, and stepped forwards again, making her back off, which made him explode with rage suddenly, shouting, 'Damn you to hell, you little bitch, stand still when I talk to you!'

'Oh . . .!' Diana cried as he caught her shoulders in a biting grip, dragging her towards him, and as her breasts brushed against his powerful muscled chest she heard herself breathe in sharply, thickly, with a rush of hot excitement as her eyes darted in panic to his.

'You see?' Conor said, pressing her against him, his strong hands moving down to her hips as he moulded her against his hard body and she wriggled breathlessly against him, inciting even sharper excitement to pulsate through her body. 'You see how completely we want each other? How much we'd both like to fall on to the nearest bed and tear each other to pieces?'

'I'm frightened!' she said breathlessly, staring hot-eyed at him as she felt the press of his hard chest and strongly muscled thighs. 'That's all—it's just fear—and why shouldn't I feel it? I know you're back for some kind of revenge . . . nothing else . . . oh, God, don't do that!'

His strong hands swept up to cover her breasts and she moaned aloud, eyes closing and mouth parting as Conor whispered thickly, 'Just frightened, my love?'

His hard mouth covered hers in a burning kiss, and suddenly they were clinging together, each making harsh sounds of excitement, their hands in each other's hair, their tongues meeting with electric heat as their bodies moved in sinuous pleasure against each other.

They fell back against the wall, eyes closed, and Conor's hands were on her breasts as she moaned wildly, her head thrown back as his hot mouth burned over her throat, and she pushed her shaking fingers through his black hair as his hard fingers stroked her erect nipple through the pink silk.

'You've thought about this!' he bit out against her mouth. 'Tell me you've thought of nothing else for six years!'

'No,' she moaned breathlessly, 'it's not true!'

'Yes, it damned well is!' he said hoarsely, and then his strong hands ripped the front of the pink silk jacket until the gold buttons flew in all directions and her breasts were bouncing free, nipples erect while she gasped in hot excitement and his thick sound of strangled pleasure made her moan as his hands clamped over her breasts and their mouths joined in red-hot, feverish kisses that almost blew her brains out.

Passion vibrated between them and in her mind it was like the trumpets sounding the apocalypse.

The danger, the horror, the fear... She felt her control slip away, felt panic flare in her mind as the reality of what was happening finally sledge-hammered through to her and she realised she stood on the very brink of chaos.

'No!' she cried hoarsely, pushing with fierce, blind panic at his broad shoulders.

Conor fell back a step, taken by surprise by the sudden ferocity of her refusal, and it gave her just enough time to run blindly for the door of the suite, wrenching it open even as he called her name angrily.

But she was out and she was free, fumbling with her pink silk jacket to do it up as she fled from him.

'Come back!' Conor's voice bit out behind her.

But she was running down the deep-pink corridor in her stockinged feet, racing blindly for sanctuary as she skidded round a corner and saw the laundry-room open.

'Come back!' Conor shouted, following her.

Diana leapt into the laundry-room, closed the door and held her breath. Minutes ticked past. Diana struggled not to break down in an agony of panic. She heard foot-steps outside, heard someone talking, and wondered how long she had been there.

Eventually, she plucked up the courage to look outside.
The corridor was deserted. Conor had evidently given
up. She felt disappointment flood her as she walked
slowly back to her suite and found the door open, the
rooms silent and deserted, the only sign of Conor's
presence the overturned table in the hall, the vase on the
floor, the red rose petals scattered...

Conor Slade had gone for the moment. But he would
be back, and Diana's mouth dried with fear and excitement at the thought of making this film with him.

How would she ever manage to stay sane?

CHAPTER TWO

ELEANOR came back with bad news that afternoon. The
contract was iron-clad, and there was nothing they could
do about Conor's appointment as director. This did not
ease Diana's state of appalling tension, and her preoc-
cupation with Conor had now blown into a dark obsession, just as it had been, right from the start.

There was no way out. It was final. He would be her
director and she his leading lady. That gave him power
over her, and Diana knew he would enjoy wielding it.
He knew how to use the whip when he held it, and my
God he really held it now!

It was almost eight o'clock. The limousine was waiting
for them downstairs. Diana got to her feet and checked
her appearance in the mirror. The pink silk strapless
evening gown glittered with a sequinned bodice, the skirt
filmy chiffon. The whole effect was dazzling, feminine,
sensual.

Did she look too sensual? Her eyes darted anxiously
over the dress. It was very sexy, but she was convinced
she could play it down, take care with her walk, keep
her face dignified...

A moment later, they were leaving the Ritz, going out
into the bright, warm scented night air. A doorman leapt
to open the limousine door for them as people stared
and pointed.

'Georgina assured me there would only be a handful of people at this party,' Eleanor said crisply as the limousine pulled away, 'and that Conor Slade would most definitely not be invited!'

'Good,' Diana said, but her eyes reflected her acute disappointment and she was furious with herself.

He wouldn't be there . . . she wouldn't see him tonight. Suddenly the party seemed dull and pointless; suddenly her beauty and the ravishing dress she wore seemed wasted. She looked broodingly out of the window of the limousine.

Why should he want to go to the party anyway? He had reappeared in her life by accident: his visit to her suite this afternoon had been a deliberate attempt to take sexual revenge on her. Not much opportunity for sexual revenge at Georgina's party tonight. He could hardly make her burn in hell for leaving him—not with guests all around them. So why should he want to go anyway?

The car was pulling into the elegant Mayfair street where Georgina Coral lived. It was jammed with parked cars—all limousines—and Diana could see lights flooding out from the big white Georgian house.

The chauffeur let them out, and they walked up the path to the front door, which was opened almost immediately by a butler with silver hair and a silver moustache.

'Madame is expecting you, of course,' he said, bowing low. 'Please follow me . . .'

They went through the long, elegant hall to the main suite of rooms, with all the doors flung open to make them seem like one. The house was overflowing with impeccably dressed guests, jazz music, and waiters carrying trays of champagne and canapés.

Diana's eyes darted obsessively around the room in search of Conor. Fool! she told herself angrily. Of course he isn't here! Stop looking for him . . . But still her eyes hunted for that dark head, that impressive height, those passionate blue eyes and that hard, hot mouth.

'Darlings!' Georgina sailed towards them like a goddess of plenty, magnificent in a purple silk evening gown that left little to the imagination as it fell below her bare shoulders. She looked like a woman in a rather *risqué* Edwardian postcard. 'You're here at last! And my devoted factotum showed you in!' She patted the butler's arm. 'Thank you, Fisher! You're an absolute poppet!'

Fisher bowed low, utterly devoted to his mistress, and disappeared.

'Everybody!' Georgina clapped her ringed hands together. 'Our guest of honour is here!'

Diana turned with a smile as conversation lulled and all heads turned to look at her, every inch the famous film star, shimmering in pink, her blonde hair cascading like silk over her bare shoulders.

'Now,' Georgina trilled, green eyes flashing, 'raise your glasses in a toast, if you please! Our star is twenty-four years old today!'

'Happy birthday, Diana!' everyone chorused, downed their champagne, and started talking again.

'Oh, to be twenty-four again...' sighed Georgina, turning to Diana with a bright smile. 'Mind you—to have to live through all that chaos again! Falling in love, flinging back and forth between ecstasy and despair... Horrors! And how obsessed one feels! The pain and the passion... My dear, I'm simply too old for it all!'

Eleanor made an angry sound beside her, blue eyes narrowing on Georgina's lovely face.

'Why, Eleanor,' said Georgina, smiling, 'I hardly noticed you there! What a lovely dress—I'm simply pea-green with envy!'

Eleanor's mouth tightened. 'Good evening, Mrs Coral.'

'Mrs Coral!' Georgina laughed, green eyes flashing. 'Heavens! I always feel I'm talking to a lawyer when someone calls me Mrs Coral! Speaking of which, Eleanor, I hear you spent a fraught afternoon with Diana's legal people.'

'We discussed the contract,' Eleanor said.

'Hmm,' Georgina drawled, smile cool. 'And what conclusion did you come to?'

'That Diana has no choice about continuing with *The Virgin and The Unicorn* under Conor Slade's direction. However——' Eleanor's head lifted, her eyes icy '—let's not beat about the bush! You may as well know that we both object to Conor Slade as director on the strongest possible grounds!'

'Which are?' Georgina asked keenly.

'That he and Diana do not get on!' said Eleanor.

'Is this true, Diana?' Georgina asked immediately, looking at her.

Diana struggled not to show any emotion. 'I don't like him very much.'

'Oh!' Georgina's brows rose. 'But, my dear, how can you not? He's so divinely attractive! Such magnetism, such energy, such intelligence! And, my dear—that scar! It hints at a murky past *par excellence*! I'm madly curious to find out where he got it.'

Diana's stomach clenched with a power-punch memory as she remembered exactly how Conor had got that scar, and how the blood had dripped from his cheek to her white blouse as she had lain beneath him.

'So very sinister,' Georgina purred, smiling, 'and so exciting. The kind of man you either love or hate.' She flicked a quick, clever look at Diana's flushed face. 'Don't you think, Diana?'

'I . . .' she could barely breathe, the memories pressing in on her '. . . I don't like Conor Slade at all! I detest him!'

'Hmm,' Georgina murmured. 'Well, that's a terrible shame, darling, because here he is!'

Diana caught her breath, head lifting in shock to stare across the room as Conor Slade's broad shoulders and terrifying height filled that white doorway.

'Doesn't he take one's breath away?' Georgina purred, taking Diana's arm. 'At least come and say hello to him!'

'You told me he wasn't invited!' Eleanor broke in fiercely, her eyes furious.

'Did I?' Georgina drawled, fluttering long lashes. 'Silly me! I quite forgot . . .' Her hand flashed with jewels on Diana's arm as she pulled her gently along after her across the deep-carpeted, thoroughly tasteful, fright-fully British drawing-room towards Conor Slade.

Diana was alive with excitement and anger, fighting everything inside as she forced herself to walk calmly to Conor and meet his hot, hellish eyes without betraying the leaping of her pulses, the quickening of her heart and the need to let her eyes race over him with unwanted desire.

'Georgina!' Conor turned to his hostess, bending his magnificent, leonine head to kiss Georgina's full mouth. 'You look ravishing as ever! I can see exactly why the Prince of Adhanne lost his head over you twenty years ago.'

'Darling! We set a torch to London and scandalised two nations!' Georgina's eyes danced. 'Please! Get your facts straight!'

Conor laughed, blue eyes flickering over her with wicked amusement. Then they flicked quickly to Diana's face and stopped her heart.

'I believe I'm being outshone,' drawled Georgina, nudging Diana forwards and saying lightly, 'You re-member our beautiful young star, don't you?'

'But, of course,' Conor said under his breath. 'How could I forget?'

'Good evening, Conor,' Diana said tensely, and almost couldn't breathe.

There was an electric silence while her heart thudded crazily in her chest and she could think of nothing but being kissed thoroughly by that hard, demanding mouth.

'Well!' Georgina smiled, satisfied. 'I'll leave you to set a torch to Mayfair and burn us all to a crisp!' She turned with a swish of purple silk and called, 'Where, oh, where is my devoted factotum?'

There was a long silence. Diana's whole body was throbbing with awareness, and she couldn't meet Conor's eyes. He was magnificent in a black evening suit, a red carnation in his lapel, his cheekbone looking bruised and jagged in this light.

'You ran out on me again,' Conor said under his breath. 'Next time I get you alone, I'll punish you for it.'

'Don't talk to me this way...!' Diana managed to choke out.

'I'll stop talking like this,' he said thickly, 'when you stop running!'

'I had to run! What else could I do?'

'Stand and face me, you little coward!' he said under his breath, his eyes burning on her face. 'Stand and admit that you're as electrified as I am and that——'

'I'm not!' she denied hotly.

'And that you want nothing more than for me to get you on the nearest bed and teach you exactly what I'll let you get away with!' His eyes blazed and narrowed. 'And, believe me, leaving me with an injunction and divorce papers isn't on the allowed list!'

'You can't tell me what I can and can't do!'

'I can if you're naked beneath me!' he said hoarsely.

'Oh...' she was almost speechless '...you wouldn't dare!'

'Oh, wouldn't I, Diana?' His eyes were hard. 'Just give me time. I'll prove it to you. And I'll enjoy it, believe me. I'll enjoy teaching you the difference between master and mistress!'

'I already know the difference!' she said bitterly. 'You taught me that a long time ago—remember?'

'Obviously, the lesson wasn't rammed into you forcibly enough,' he said, mouth hard as he stared angrily into her eyes and enjoyed her harsh intake of breath at his insolent words. His gaze slid to her tense body, to her full breasts and the dazzling pink sequins of her bodice. 'That's a lovely dress. Did you wear it for me?'

Her face flushed with hot angry colour and she spat out, 'No!'

Conor laughed softly, blue eyes mocking.

'I didn't!' she said angrily, lifting her head. 'I didn't give you a thought while I was dressing!'

'And when you were undressing?'

'I never give you a thought at all,' she said fiercely, face burning, 'day or night!'

His mouth hardened. 'You will in future, Diana. By the time I'm through with you you'll be so completely my mistress that you'll think of me every time you see yourself naked!'

Diana's mouth dried and she said breathlessly, 'Seeing you again, Conor, has only made me hate you more than I did six years ago.'

'That's exactly what I'm banking on,' he said bitingly, and their eyes warred in a cataclysmic silence as Diana saw him tearing her to pieces in an outburst of frenzied passion at some not too distant point in the future, and felt her body begin to shake at the prospect.

'Darlings!' Georgina swooped down on them again, her devoted factotum at her side with a silver tray of champagne glasses. 'What a very passionate argument you're having! But may I rain on your very dazzling parade and inform you that Eleanor is currently making her way over here?'

Diana turned, catching her breath to see Eleanor moving towards them.

'She has a singularly determined look on her face,' said Georgina. 'I advocate an immediate discussion on my divine new Rossetti!'

Conor's hard mouth twisted in a derisive smile. 'The one above the mantelpiece? It's a fake and you know it!'

'My dear, that's hardly the point!' Georgina laughed. 'After all, one's only supposed to look at it and feel passionate! Does it matter if the great artist him-self——? Ah! Eleanor! Wonderful to see you joining in at last! You really ought to mingle more!'

Eleanor looked glacially at Diana. 'I feel Mr Slade is monopolising Diana. Shouldn't she be circulating?'

'Yes, you're quite right, Eleanor,' Conor drawled coolly, startling Diana, who looked up at him with a shocked stare as he finally relinquished his hold on her hand and gave Eleanor a cool, sardonic smile. 'Take her away and circulate her. I must have a quick word with our hostess...'

He turned his back on them both, and Diana felt her lips part with surprise as she stared at the back of his powerful shoulders, and the black hair that curled against the top of his smart white shirt-collar.

'Come along, Diana,' Eleanor said icily, 'I've just been introduced to a first-class lawyer in the film world.'

'I don't want to talk to any lawyers,' Diana said, turning from Conor and moving away, her stomach churning with nausea at the impact of not only his presence, but what he had said to her.

'He could help us,' Eleanor pressed, frowning.

Diana looked up, eyes wild. 'Help us...yes...' Her eyes focused as she looked at her guardian properly and said, 'You mean with this? With Conor?'

'Of course. He's a lawyer, isn't he?'

Diana's eyes darted and she said, 'But how can we even ask? This is Georgina's party! It would be bad-mannered to ask her own lawyer about——'

'He's not *her* lawyer,' Eleanor said at once, 'he came with a starlet, and nobody even knows him.'

There was a brief silence. Diana thought fast, then gave a quick nod, saying, 'OK. I'll speak to him. But we must be discreet...'

Eleanor looked relieved, and a moment later they were walking across the crowded drawing-room, through the double oak doors that led to the library, and up to a circle of two or three people drinking champagne.

'Ah,' Eleanor extended a slender hand, 'Mr Sinclair!'

Diana smiled as she was introduced and shook hands with the lawyer, listening as Eleanor made vague references to the contract without specifying whose it was.

The dreary legal conversation flowed on and on. Diana drank her champagne, mouth dry as ashes as she remembered what Conor had said. He was only trying to unnerve her! Trying to latch in on her Achilles heel, which he knew only too well, and get his revenge on her.

He knows exactly where to aim, she thought as the hair on the back of her neck prickled and she constantly

looked round in search of him, in search of his hard face
and hot blue eyes and the turn of that determined jaw
as he, too, looked for her.

Forever, it seemed, she stood in polite silence while
Eleanor and the lawyer talked. The conversation was
going to be fruitless. She knew that without bothering
to listen.

But the evening itself was growing more and more
fraught, and her eyes met Conor's across the room...her
mind overflowed with forbidden images of his mouth
on hers, his long hands on her nude body. It was intolerable. She had to do something...had to get away...had
to stop him doing this to her...

'Ah!' Georgina appeared just as the clock struck ten.
'There you are!'

Eleanor looked at her icily. 'Georgina. How nice.'

'Eleanor, I simply must introduce you to my new arrival.' Georgina determinedly took Eleanor's slender
arm. 'He's a politician and his father was Winston
Churchill's best friend. You'll get on famously...'

'Really?' Eleanor was at once intrigued, allowing
Georgina to lead her away. 'But how marvellous! Does
he remember Churchill?'

'Oh, frightfully well! He used to sit under the table
and eavesdrop when Churchill came to dinner...'

Diana clutched her champagne, watching them dis-
appear and looking at once for Conor, as though he were
a magnet and she an iron filing, drawn inexorably
together across time and space, love and hate.

The lawyer started to speak to her, but his starlet at
once appeared in a temper and dragged him away.

Diana looked across that crowded room directly into
Conor's eyes and started to shake. She had drunk too
much. Her face was flushed and hot; there were too many
people in the room. She needed a breath of fresh air and
she needed to get away from Conor.

Putting her glass down, she started to walk coolly
towards the door.

'Running away so soon?' drawled Conor's dark, satanic voice as he blocked her path with his powerful

chest, and as she raised her wild blue gaze to his face she saw he was angry and determined.

'I don't want to talk to you, Conor!' she said under her breath. 'I want fresh air...I want to be alone. I——'

'Very Greta Garbo,' he drawled, 'only she didn't have your capacity for making such passionate enemies, of which I am one.' His strong fingers curled like iron bands around her wrist. 'If you want fresh air, you shall have it; but you shall have it with me.'

'No!' She tried to pull away from him. 'I told you— I want to be alone!'

'Not while there's life left in me, Diana!' he said tightly, eyes hating her. 'Now, come on!' He pulled her wrist and she stumbled after him, dwarfed by his sheer strength.

She couldn't cause a scene; not with so many people around. Eleanor was deep in conversation with a distinguished silver-haired gentleman, and nobody noticed Conor Slade taking such blatant mastery over Diana Sullivan.

There were one or two people lounging in the hall, talking indolently as cooler air fanned their faces from the open front door. It was dark now, and the Mayfair street was ravishing in the warm summer night; streetlights shining on lush green trees, giving their leaves an unearthly glow, the limousines glittering under moonlight and the sound of London traffic on Park Lane a distant throb.

'Still frightened out of your mind?' Conor asked softly as he held her in the doorway, towering over her, his hand still clamped over her wrist.

'I'm always frightened when you're around,' she gave an angry laugh, courage in her eyes, 'because I know you'll stop at nothing to get what you want!'

'I'm glad you know who you're dealing with.'

'I've always known it!' she said under her breath. 'I just wasn't strong enough to fight it the first time around. But I'm twenty-four now, Conor, and I can stand up to anything you try to dish out, you brute!'

He laughed under his breath, eyes flicking to her mouth. 'Brute, am I? I suppose you'd prefer it if I just forgave and forgot?'

'I'd prefer it if you just went away and left me alone!'

'So you keep telling me,' he said tightly, unsmiling, 'but I'm afraid that's not the way the cookie's going to crumble this time, and you might as well face it.'

Diana looked at him, her head lifted, blonde hair fanning back gently from her beautiful face, and her blue eyes signalled the beginnings of acceptance, and the beginning of a fight to the death.

'It seems I have no choice,' she said under her breath.

'None.' He nodded, unsmiling, then said coolly, 'Shall we walk?'

For some reason, she nodded too, and said, 'OK.'

They walked slowly along the path and out through the gate. A few birds were still singing. The streetlights shone gold on her creamy skin, the pink sequins on her dress flashing.

'You still walk like a siren,' he said, watching her out of the corner of his eye as her hips swayed.

Diana flushed. 'I didn't know I ever did.'

'Sure,' he replied sardonically. 'That's why you went into films and became an international sex symbol!'

Her mouth tightened. 'I went into films by accident.'

'Oh?' His brows rose as they walked coolly along the night-time street. 'Tell me about it.'

Diana shrugged slim bare shoulders. 'I . . . was lucky, that's all. My Uncle Claudius had a lot of contacts in the film world, and I happened to meet one of them in New York. He took a shine to me, and——'

'And the rest is history, as they say,' drawled Conor, eyes narrowing as he halted, looking down at her. 'How much of a shine did this movie mogul take to you, Diana?'

She frowned, saying, 'Well—enough to give me a screen test and a——'

'Casting-couch test?' he asked under his breath, eyes hard.

'No!'

His mouth tightened as he gripped her arm with hard fingers. 'Tell me the truth! Did he test you on the couch as well as—— ?'

'No, he didn't!' she said angrily. 'What do you think I am?'

He breathed unevenly, studying her face, then he nodded, and thrust one hand in his black trouser pocket. 'OK,' he said deeply, 'I believe you.'

Diana studied him, holding her breath for a moment, then she asked the question she had been burning to ask for years: 'And you? How did you end up in this...crazy business?'

The blue eyes were lit with cynical amusement. 'A similar connection. An ex-girlfriend of mine is a film actress, and she suggested me to Jack Coral—Georgina's father—when he was looking for an action director.'

Jealousy shot through her like hot knives and she said tartly, 'I can almost see the words "casting-couch" lit up on your forehead!'

He laughed coolly, and drawled, 'Jealous, my love?'

'No!' Her face ran with hot colour as she lifted her head and met his mocking gaze. 'Not at all. I just want you to see how despicable your double standards are!'

'I'd already split with Talia by the time I made that first film with Coral, and I——'

'Talia!' She sucked in her breath, eyes wide with sudden appalled realisation. 'You—you don't mean Talia Hite?'

He inclined his dark head, unsmiling.

'But she's my co-star in this film!' Diana breathed, eyes incredulous with jealousy. 'You must know that!'

'I know it,' he said lazily, a hard smile on his mouth. 'Why—are you going to be tortured with jealousy by the sight of my directing her?'

'Oh, you're just dying to try and make me jealous, aren't you?'

'Damned right!' he said softly, watching her through heavy lids.

There was a brief, tense silence. The wind lifted her hair gently and as she looked into his determined face she realised quite what a battle this film was going to be.

'Talia's a very beautiful woman,' Conor said softly, watching her closely. 'Desirable...passionate...sexy...'

'All right!' she said tightly, hating him. 'We all know what a great witch she'll make in the film!'

He laughed out loud, eyes sliding with wicked amusement to her mouth as he drawled, 'Bitch!'

She lifted her brows haughtily and said, 'I wasn't being spiteful. What I say is true. She's suited to the part and——'

'So will you be,' he cut in softly, 'by the time I've finished with you. But here I am...making such grand promises...and I haven't even started delivering them yet.' Dark brows rose as he took his hand from his pocket and continued, 'It's never too late to start...'

Suddenly she saw the flash of silver keys in his hand as his other hand shot out and gripped her wrist, blue eyes blazing at her as he leant to a car door and unlocked it quickly.

'No...!' she began inaudibly, struggling.

'Get in the car, Diana!' he said under his breath, forcing her to the open door, his hands on her bare shoulders.

'No! Get your hands off me! You're mad! You're——'

The car door swung open. 'I said get in!' he demanded tightly. 'Or do you want me to pick you up and throw you in?'

Diana looked back at the house, heart thumping with panic. It was too far for her to run. The party too noisy for a scream to be heard.

'Weighing up your options?' Conor said quietly behind her, his mouth against her hair. 'You'll never get back there. We're too far. You may as well accept defeat and get in.'

She was suddenly terrified, staring at the car with wide eyes, unable to move.

Conor's hands suddenly slid under her legs and he lifted her in his arms with ease, ignoring her stifled gasp

as he thrust her into the front seat of the steel-blue Jaguar
XJS, slamming the door on her cries of protest and
walking around to the other side before she had time to
scramble out.

'No, you don't!' he growled, dragging her back into
the car as he slid behind the steering-wheel. He leant
over and slammed her door shut again. 'You just sit tight
and think about what you're going to say when we get
back to my place, because, believe me, Diana, we are
going to have one hell of a conversation!'

The XJS flared into life and they shot away with a
roar from that quiet Mayfair street.

Diana was trembling. A cold sweat had broken out
on her skin. Her hands were damp as they twisted in her
lap, and the chiffon scarf at her throat was sticking to
her as that hot pulse throbbed in her body.

'Where... where is your place?' She tried to sound
strong.

'Chelsea,' Conor replied, whizzing past Marble Arch,
lit up by floodlights. 'I have an apartment on the
harbour-front.'

'Chelsea!'

'Hmm,' he said with a cool smile, 'the film industry
pays more than the SAS!'

'You always said you'd be rich one day...'

'And I am,' he said flatly. 'Very rich. You were right,
my dear.' One long finger slid suddenly, intimately along
her slim thigh, making her quiver. 'My taste for danger
has paid me handsomely. You used to say it would all
make sense one day. And it has.'

'Your films have all been action pictures,' she said,
struggling to turn the conversation away from more personal subjects, 'and nobody else in the business can touch
you...'

'Nobody else in the business was trained in the SAS,'
he said gruffly.

'So it all makes sense...' she said huskily, watching
him. 'I'm glad, Conor. For you. But——'

'No, you're not,' he said, mouth hard. 'You're just a
survivor from way back. And right now you're in a tight

spot. You'll say anything to survive. Anything at all. Anything to defuse my anger and keep me at arm's length...' He touched her thigh with one strong hand and said deeply, 'Your back's against the wall, Diana.'

'Stop touching my leg like that!' She slapped his hand angrily.

'Your thigh!' he mocked softly, watching her through black lashes. 'And you're beginning to feel it!'

'No!' she denied hotly, staring out of the window as the car sped along the King's Road. 'I don't feel anything! Nothing at all!'

He laughed under his breath, and the car slowed as he indicated right and turned into a narrow road which led to a long private mews. Little white mews houses dotted the uneven road. Flowers hung from one front porch, the roofs were black, and it looked expensively chic.

Conor stopped the steel-blue XJS, plunged out the lights and turned to look at her in the darkened interior, his blue eyes glittering with the thirst for revenge.

'We're here, my love!' he said softly, and her heart lurched with panic. 'Time to face the music!'

She was breathless as she met his intent gaze. 'Is it a pastoral symphony, Conor?'

'No,' he said under his breath, 'a bloodthirsty opera by Puccini.'

'I suppose we all die in the third act?'

'I don't know,' he said deeply, 'but there are an awful lot of climaxes before the curtain comes down.'

She stumbled out of the car, breathless, and Conor stepped out too, tall and dark and inexorably menacing as he crossed the private mews, led her by the wrist to his house, and opened the white wooden front door without a word.

He thrust her in through the open door, walked in behind her and closed the door, leaning against it and watching her.

It was pitch-black. Her heart was banging. All she could see was the glitter of his eyes.

'Put the light on,' she whispered thickly. 'I ... I can't see you!'

His powerful shadow moved. 'I don't want you to see me,' he said softly. 'That's the whole point. I just want you to feel.'

'I do feel!' she said angrily. 'I feel extremely resentful that you've bullied me over here! Now, please—put the light on!'

'You sound as jumpy as a cornered cat to me!' he mocked softly in the darkness.

Panic made her say hotly, 'Come near me and you'll find out just how sharp my claws can be!'

'Don't tempt me. I've never forgotten the scratch-marks you left on my back!'

'Oh ...!' Her whole body was alive with heat. 'You—swine!'

His laughter made every hair on her body stand on end. 'Still adamant that you feel nothing for me?'

She breathed in the darkness, not daring to speak in case he did what they both knew was on the cards: took her in his arms and kissed the life out of her.

She had to say something to defuse this danger. 'I just feel—nervous here in the dark with you, Conor,' she managed at last, her voice rough with panic. 'Please put the light on and let me see your face.'

There was a silence, then he moved, a switch was thrown and light flooded the room. Diana flinched from it, eyes closing, then she looked at him through her lashes and wondered how any man had the right to be so mouthwateringly gorgeous. Georgina was right; that scar only heightened his disturbing brand of sex appeal, and as she looked into his eyes her extreme nervousness showed on her face.

'You look as if you're going to the scaffold,' Conor said tonelessly, mouth hard.

'It's how I feel,' she answered honestly.

A sardonic smile twisted his mouth. 'Well ... I guess that's better than nothing. At least I still have some effect on you, even if it's not the desired one.' He moved away from her, saying coolly, 'Drink? I have some vermouth—I remember you always used to drink that.'

'Did I?' she asked huskily, the memory evoked suddenly poignant, though she fought it even as she watched the back of his black head. 'It seems such a long time ago...'

'Six years is a long time,' Conor said, flipping open the mahogany cabinet, and beyond his dark head the lights of Chelsea harbour glittered through the vast bay windows.

She looked around the living-room, her eyes adjusting to the light. Conor had done very well indeed, she realised, recognising the unmistakable signs of not only wealth but exceptional taste. The dark green rugs on the polished wooden floor, the mahogany coffee-table with a Chinese silver cigar-box on it, the paintings on the wall reflecting an eclectic, passionate and wildly romantic man behind the tough, almost brutal exterior.

Conor came back to her, a glass of vermouth in one hand, a shot of whisky in the other.

'Thank you,' Diana said huskily, taking her vermouth with a strong sense of *déjà vu* and turning away from him to hide it by saying, 'I was just admiring your paintings. I particularly like this one...'

'It's called "Celtic Dawn",' Conor said flatly, watching her, narrow-eyed, as she walked to the clear painting of a circle of primitive stones. 'Don't change the subject.'

'What subject?' she asked, trembling.

'Six years,' he said, mouth hard.

There was a silence, then Diana returned, 'I—I don't see what there is to be said. Not after the divorce and——'

'When did you dye your hair?' he asked flatly.

This time, the silence was even more tense.

'I...' she ran a hand through her blonde silken tresses '...I can't really remember. It was such a——'

'Six years ago?' he drawled tightly, eyes hard.

She flushed angrily. 'Uncle Claudius's friend in New York said I'd get much better roles if I went blonde!'

He nodded, mouth cynical. 'Blondes have more scope?'

'Something like that, yes!' Her blue eyes were resentful. 'Besides—I think I look better blonde. So does everyone else. It suits my colouring; everyone says so.'

'I don't,' said Conor.

'No,' she looked at him angrily, 'you preferred me when I was a brunette not two months out of school and stupid enough to fall into your bed without understanding what was——' She broke off with a gasp, staring at him, unable to believe she had said that. He looked quite shocked, too, and for a second or two they just stood there staring at each other in tense silence.

'Well!' Conor said under his breath, blue eyes hard. 'That's quite a speech, Diana. Quite a condemnation.'

'I . . .' she looked away, flushing ' . . . it's how I feel, Conor.'

'And you really believe it? I mean—you believe it's the truth?'

'Of course!' Her head came up, a frown on her brow. 'I was seventeen when we met. Seventeen and very sheltered. I didn't know what you wanted to——' She flushed hotly, avoiding his eyes. 'I mean—I didn't understand what was happening, Conor! You must see that!'

'I married you, Diana,' he said under his breath. 'Surely that changes everything?'

'Not for me,' she said hoarsely. 'Not when you come back like this—talking of nothing but sex, staring at me like that . . . I . . .'

'Like what?' he demanded harshly.

'You know . . .' she said, looking at him, blue eyes fierce. 'The way you always used to look at me. As though you wanted to . . . to . . .' she found herself almost unable to go on, but forced herself to say it angrily, her voice shaking ' . . . to tear me to pieces!'

Conor watched her in silence for a second, then raised his glass to his hard mouth and took a shot of whisky. He put the glass down on the table and replied gruffly, 'I can't deny it. That's exactly what I want to do.' He raked a hand through his hair, saying tightly, 'It's just another facet of the same emotion, Diana. And we both feel it, whether you're prepared to admit it or not.'

She was breathless, staring at him. 'What emotion, Conor?'

His lashes flickered. A cynical smile twisted his mouth. 'Passionate attraction,' he drawled lazily. 'What else?'

Disappointment hit her like a sledge-hammer, sending her heart plummeting, but she refused to acknowledge her feelings and concentrated on just remaining calm as much as possible: a very difficult feat when Conor Slade was within a fifty-mile radius of her.

'Passionate attraction,' she repeated through dry lips. 'I see. So what I said was true—you only want——'

'To make love to you,' Conor agreed under his breath, 'but don't call it sex, because it goes deeper than that, Diana: way deeper. It goes right down to the darkest part of your soul: the part that matches mine.'

'Conor, really!' she said in breathless fear, laughing huskily to hide her nervousness. 'I hope you know what you're talking about, because I certainly don't!' She sipped her vermouth, spilling some so that it ran down her chin and she clucked her tongue nervously, putting the glass down.

'Wait!' Conor moved towards her, eyes staring. 'I'll do that for——'

'It's nothing!' she protested, backing off. 'I just spilled——'

'I said I'll do it!' he told her under his breath, and his hands held her wrists in an iron grip as he towered over her, bending his dark head while she stared into his eyes, and slowly he licked the warm vermouth from her chin while she caught her breath; slowly his tongue slid up to her lips and his hot blue gaze met hers as he said thickly, 'Perhaps we should spill some more—hmm?' His hand reached for her glass.

'No!' Diana shot away from him as though burnt, her eyes panic-stricken. 'Conor, for God's sake! How much louder can my refusal get?'

'It'll never be loud enough,' he murmured, watching her, 'not while I see that look in your eyes. Do you think I don't know how you feel? Do you think me a fool?'

'I divorced you!' she said fiercely. 'Doesn't that mean anything to you?'

'You divorced yourself!' he bit out, blue eyes blazing suddenly, and, as Diana stared at him in the silence that followed, she felt her heartbeat turn into his and knew he was as deeply, desperately involved with her as she was with him.

'I . . .' her voice was shredded with the force of her hated passion ' . . . I don't know what you're——'

'You know as well as I do that we're two halves of the same soul!' he grated, staring at her. 'Don't you feel it even now?' He came towards her, mouth determined. 'As we stand in the same room together, see each other face to face, touch each other for the first time in years . . .'

'I left you behind!' she said fiercely. 'I left it all behind!'

'You just dyed your hair blonde and ran away from me!' he bit out, eyes fierce. 'That's all, Diana! You just changed yourself into another woman . . .' He took her chin in one strong hand and thrust it up to meet his gaze as he said tightly, 'And I'm here to change you back!'

'You can't go back!' she whispered, mouth quivering under that intense stare. 'You know that better than anyone, Conor!'

'OK,' he said with a sardonic smile, 'I'll change you forwards. How's that? Strip you of all this . . . this artifice, and give you absolute freedom of——'

'I don't want to change!' she said angrily. 'I'm happy the way I——'

'Oh?' he demanded angrily. 'Happy, are you?' His hand left her chin, slid downward, slid to her white throat where the pulse beat wildly at his touch. 'And how many times have you been made love to since we split up? Hmm?' His hand moved down to touch her breast slowly, teasingly, as he murmured, 'How many lovers have there been?'

'What has that to do with happiness?' she demanded, giving an angry laugh.

'Oh, a great deal, Diana!' he said under his breath, eyes narrowing. 'Who holds you at night in your lonely bed? Who kisses you full on the mouth when you wake up? Who makes you weep with pleasure when——?'

'It's all just sex, isn't it, Conor?' she said bitterly, hating him, loving him, flung constantly between the two every time she saw him. 'And that's all it ever was!'

'It's life!' he said bitingly, blue eyes angry. 'And you're supposed to be living it! Not locking yourself up in an artificial world with an artificial hair colour and an artificial love-life!'

'I'm an actress,' she defended herself angrily.

'You're a living photograph!' he said tightly. 'And there's a big difference, Diana! Where's the girl I met? Where's she gone?'

'Let go of me, you——'

'Where is she?' he bit out, and his hands took her head between them, his fingers thrusting into her blonde hair as he stared into her face and said harshly, 'Where's that brave, beautiful brunette? The one who wanted to act on the stage? The one who loved *Hamlet* and Chekhov and——?'

'Adolescent dreams!' she said hoarsely. 'Let go! You're hurting——'

'The woman who turned to fire in my arms?' he continued, staring at her. 'The woman who unleashed every demon in my soul and returned them all with such passion? You made me complete! You made my life worth living! You were my other half and you tore me apart when you left...oh, God, you little bitch, how could you leave me like that? How could you leave me?' He was shouting as he finished, and then he seemed to lose control, giving a fierce cry as he took her shoulders and whirled her with him towards the couch, his eyes manic.

'No!' She was facing dark chaos, stumbling backwards, breathing erratically. 'No, you can't!'

'Oh, yes!' he said thickly, and grabbed her by the wrists. 'Yes, I damned well can, and what's more—I'm damned well going to!'

'Let me go...!' She struggled uselessly, and his hard hands pushed her backwards, back until she fell on the couch behind her with a thud and a gasp.

'Lie back!' Conor bit out under his breath as his shadow obliterated her and his hard thighs pressed her down into the couch, his grim mouth inches from hers. 'Lie back and think of Ireland!'

'Oh, God...!' she gasped hoarsely, and then she was moaning beneath the onslaught of that mouth, her lips parting with the demanding pressure until his tongue slid through and her body leapt in wild response. His tongue withdrew and she caught her breath, but it snaked back, snaked in and out and she was reeling under the fast, fiery pressure of his expertise, her thighs twisting against his as he pressed her down with his body, and one strong hand slid up over her belly, up towards her breasts and the zip of her sequinned dress.

The zip flared down and she moaned, struggling for control, but he had been too fast and too clever, and she felt herself hurtle into that dark, chaotic passion with him.

'Yes!' Conor was saying gruffly as he fondled her bare breasts. 'Yes, you want me, you little bitch, and now you're going to get me!'

His strong hands pulled the absurd pink dress down to her waist, and, as she gasped and whispered pleas for mercy, so his strong hands ruthlessly stroked her breasts, her erect nipples, and when his dark head bent in that dangerous, passionate darkness to fasten his hot mouth on her nipple she gave a hoarse cry of agonised ecstasy, arching against him, her hands thrusting in his hair.

'Conor...!' Her voice was harsh, shaking, foreign. 'Oh, God...no more...no more!'

He said not a word in reply, just ruined her with his expertise, his eyes ruthless as his hands slid to her thighs, inciting sexual frenzy. She cried out in hoarse protest, writhing beneath him, clutching his shoulders, helpless in her passion and her weakness as she whispered against his strong neck, 'Please ... please ... please!'

There was a silence so thick with excitement that Diana believed herself to be on the brink of a terrible abyss, her heart pounding so hard that she had to cling to her sanity with both hands, terrified she would fall and be burnt to death in the flames of her sin.

Conor studied her in the darkness, breathing harshly, still silent, his eyes glittering with a fever she remembered all too well ...

'I can't!' Diana said rawly, eyes hating him. 'Can't!'

'You mean you won't!' came the hoarse reply.

'I mean I can't!' she repeated, and suddenly clung to his powerful body, her cheek pressed against his hard chest, and the sound of his thudding heart was felt deep in her own soul. 'It's just an attraction ... just a physical attraction and I can't give in to it!'

He breathed harshly above her blonde head and said deeply, 'You will give in to it, Diana! Sooner or later. Or do I have to remind you that we're going to be cooped up in a château in the Loire Valley for the next fortnight together?'

Stiffening, she stared at his chest, at the white shirt, and said, 'We're working together ... of course ... oh, God, I'd forgotten ...'

'Yes,' he said, and his hand tangled in her hair as he drew her head back to look at him, 'and I'm your director. That gives me the whip-hand, Diana, and I intend to use it!'

'To abuse it, you mean!' she said fiercely, hating him. 'And, believe me, if I could do anything to get out of doing this picture now, I'd jump at it!'

His eyes were mocking. 'But you can't—can you? You're ...' His gaze slid to her bare breasts and he ran one long finger over her erect nipple as he said under his breath, 'Powerless!'

Diana moistened her lips, and his eyes followed the little movement, then his head swooped and he kissed her, kissed her with such burning passion that she found herself falling back again, moaning helplessly as his hands moved over her breasts and she felt those demons rise up in her as he had said they did: always had, always would . . .

'I like to see you powerless, Diana!' he said hoarsely as his head moved and his hot mouth closed over her nipple. 'It makes the last six years bearable . . .'

'Don't!' she whispered, clutching his head in tortuous pleasure and hating herself even as the sharp needles of excitement pierced her. 'Don't!'

'Held in check by that damned injunction!' he bit out, his hands moving to her thighs as his mouth ravaged her breast. 'You little bitch, do you have any idea how I felt? I wanted to kill you . . . I hated you . . . hated you so bitterly . . . and this is the only thing that kept me alive . . .'

'Oh, God . . .' she moaned as he pressed her molten body against his hardness. 'Conor . . .'

'Knowing that one day,' he murmured against her mouth, 'I could come back and make you suffer: as I suffered. Make you feel powerless, trapped, angry, jealous, driven half crazy with frustration!'

'Conor, please!' she whispered shakingly against the excitement induced by those strong, dark-haired hands and powerless to stop them. 'I must get back to the hotel before Eleanor! I must! If she gets there first and finds I'm not there——'

'You're a grown woman,' he said flatly, his mouth on her throat. 'You can stay out after nine o'clock.'

'No!' she said forcibly and clutched his broad shoulders. She had to get out of here, get away from him and his deliberate temptation. 'Please take me back! I must be there before Eleanor; I must!'

There was a pause. Conor lifted his head and looked at her with a frown, his heart thudding as he studied her in deep thought and said nothing.

She moistened her lips and said huskily, 'I must get back for Eleanor.'

'You must get back for Eleanor,' Conor said slowly, and then he released her, standing, eyes narrowed. He looked at her suddenly with eyes wide, and then he looked away, running a hand through his hair and drawing a harsh breath, thrusting his hands deep in his trouser pockets.

Diana watched him. 'Conor?'

'I'll make a deal with you!' he said harshly, turning to look at her, mouth tight. 'I'll take you back to the Ritz now. But if I do, then you must do something in return for me.' He stepped towards her, eyes fierce. 'You must have dinner with me on our first night at Château Balzac.'

Diana stiffened, recoiling instinctively from the idea of spending any time alone with him. 'Dinner?' Her eyes watched him warily. 'On Monday?'

'The first night,' he agreed. 'Filming doesn't begin until Tuesday, and even then at twilight for the first big scene. We'll be able to have a late night on Monday without repercussions. Well?' The blue eyes studied her angrily. 'Is it a deal?'

'Yes, of course,' she said angrily, because she had no choice and they both knew it.

'You'd better keep to that deal,' Conor suddenly strode towards her, bending swiftly, his eyes fierce as he watched her frightened face, 'or I swear to God I'll make you regret it!'

'I understand!' she said fiercely. 'There's no need to underline it!'

'If you try to back out of it, I'll give you the penalty full blast!' he said tightly.

'I don't doubt it!' she answered, heart thumping hotly at the very thought.

'I'll make your head spin!' he said, and one hand moved ruthlessly to cover her breast, enjoying her outraged gasp as she stared at him helplessly. 'I'll make love to you until you beg for mercy! Got it?'

'Yes!' she said fiercely, heart banging with anger and excitement. 'Yes!'

His eyes glittered. 'We'll be together in that château for at least a fortnight, Diana. There'll be other people about ... but we won't notice them, will we, Diana? Not if you disobey me and force me to drive you mad with excitement!'

'I...I won't disobey you!' she said thickly, hating him.

He watched her for a second with narrowed eyes, then he straightened, moving away towards the front door. He went out, and Diana got up after a moment, her legs shaky as she followed him.

The steel-blue XJS was open and waiting for her. Conor's eyes slid to her bruised mouth, tousled hair, ravaged body, as she slipped nervously into the front seat.

'Better repair your lipstick,' he drawled, walking round to the driver's side, 'unless you want Eleanor to guess just exactly what her angelic little ward has been up to!'

'Oh!' Nothing could have jolted her more. If she got back like this, she would look like her real mother, the mother she must never, ever resemble. Not while Eleanor was there to see it. Not while Eleanor was there to point a finger and say: you look just like Allannah Sullivan.

'Personally,' Conor drawled, watching her as she drew out her lipstick, 'I think you look as sexy as hell like this.'

Her eyes shot to him angrily. 'Nobody asked your opinion!'

His smile was mocking. 'You look as though you've just been made love to...and by someone who knows how!' He touched her mouth with one long finger. 'I'll make sure you look like this every day in France...'

'I need a mirror,' she said, tight-lipped and hating him. 'May I use the rear-view-mirror for a——?'

Conor flipped open the cosmetics mirror in the passenger dashboard. Diana stared at it, jealousy suddenly burning her like a knife tipped with acid twisting in her heart. Cosmetics mirror . . . women . . . other women...other women in this big powerful car with this big powerful man beside them, telling them to repair their make-up after his passion had wreaked havoc on them...

Had he wreaked havoc on Talia Hite? she wondered bitterly.

Oh, she despised herself! Don't feel it, she told herself furiously, applying the pink lipstick to her ravaged mouth: don't even think about it! Conor Slade always was a handsome devil—he's probably had hundreds of women and can't remember their names!

The engine flared. The Jaguar shot on to the King's Road, lights flickering from the clubs and restaurants and boutiques on to Conor's dark, jagged-boned face.

She suddenly remembered their wedding night, when they had dined in the only restaurant for miles and the pretty Irish girl with red hair had smiled at Conor, flirting with him openly. She remembered the fierce jealousy she had felt then and the daggers she had looked at the girl as she had flounced off.

Nothing changes, she thought bitterly. Not my feelings for Conor or his feelings for me. But this wild, passionate love between them would destroy them both unless it was stopped: unless it was strangled and killed and cut off forever. She could not go into that chaotic darkness—no! Not for all the ecstasy he offered her.

Her eyes flicked to his hard, handsome face in the darkened interior of the car. They would be alone at Château Balzac for a fortnight. Even though other people would be there, they would still be under the same roof, flung together all day and night...

Would she be able to keep him at arm's length?

CHAPTER THREE

CHÂTEAU BALZAC baked a warm dusty beige under the Loire Valley sun, the three wings of the castle unfolding like a tryptych on an altar of bleached yellow grass.

Grey leaded turrets pierced an azure sky and the land shimmered and was distorted in a heat haze as they drove towards it. The high black gates swung wide. The limousine swept up the drive, bleached and pebble-strewn with tall thin trees lining it like footmen welcoming Diana to her dream—her nightmare. They parked in front of the magnificent double oak doors. The crew were here already—she could see their cars and vans and long lorries filled with equipment.

'Welcome, darlings!' cried Georgina, sailing out of the château like Madame de Pompadour, her chestnut hair piled high in glorious curls, her white sun-dress flaunting her bosom and jewels and splendid creamy skin.

'Georgina!' Diana stepped out of the limousine, blonde hair bright in the sun. 'Isn't this a fabulous place?' Her eyes shone as she gazed at the bleached beige-gold bricks of the castle walls.

'Home sweet château!' trilled Georgina, flinging her arms wide. 'And, my dear, you simply must see the landscaped gardens at the back! So like Versailles!'

'Oh, gosh; I love Versailles!' Diana said, pale blue dress floating in the warm breeze as she walked up the steps with Georgina.

'If only it weren't always full of ghastly tourists,' sighed Georgina.

They walked into the vast marble hallway of the château.

'Just put the trunks down,' Eleanor was saying crisply to the chauffeur. 'No, not like that, you imbecile!'

'Just look at this!' Diana stared in awe at the high-ceilinged hallway, the magnificent crystal chandelier swaying in the breeze above a sweeping marble staircase.

'Isn't it divine?' Georgina's green eyes were wistful. 'My grandparents lived in a similar fashion. High ceilings, ancestral paintings, masked balls, servants everywhere...' She gave a deep sigh. 'Ah, well—we must accept our destinies and make the best of them.'

'Yes...' Diana thought of Conor and of destiny and shivered.

'Conor,' said Georgina, displaying remarkable tele-pathic gifts, 'wants to shoot one of the love scenes in the stables! Isn't he wicked?'

Diana tensed. 'He...he's already here, then?'

'Arrived last night.' Georgina nodded. 'Ah...' she turned her glorious head '...here's Eleanor! Match-lessly elegant as always. Eleanor, darling—welcome to the Loire Valley.'

'Thank you, Georgina,' Eleanor said coldly and turned to the chauffeur. 'Kindly handle those trunks with care.'

'You must be exhausted,' Georgina said at once. 'I'll show you to your rooms *tout de suite*. Do enjoy the stairs—one must sweep up them to do them justice...' and she swept majestically up the cool pale green marble steps, every footstep an echo that resounded in the superb acoustics of Château Balzac.

The corridors of the three-winged château were stunning. High-ceilinged, marble, with antique furniture dotted about from time to time along with exquisite paintings.

'What on earth possessed the Balzac family to give up their magnificent home,' Eleanor commented, 'to a film crew?'

'Money, darling!' trilled Georgina. 'What else?' She sailed ahead of them and flung open a tall golden oak door, saying, 'Diana's boudoir!'

'Oh...!' Diana walked into the pale gold room, lit by bright sunlight from the open french doors. A four-poster bed dominated the room, carved in golden oak and hung with ivory lace, the dressing-table, chest of drawers and wardrobe all antiques, and made from golden oak with gold handles.

'I say!' Eleanor was, for once, awestruck as she too moved into the centre of the room and said, 'This really is exceptional!'

'Hmm.' Georgina smiled coolly. 'Your room is quite super, too, Eleanor. Won't you follow me?'

Eleanor turned, black brows lifting. 'I take it I'm in the connecting room?'

'Why, no!' Georgina said, green eyes shocked. 'Cast and crew only on this floor! You're on the second floor, Eleanor!'

'What?' Eleanor was icy, her body erect, pearls gleaming at her ears, the black chignon impeccable.

'I'm so sorry, Eleanor.' Georgina clasped her ringed hands together, very cool. 'If you wish to take it up with Mr Slade, I'm sure he'll be only too happy to discuss the problem.'

Diana stiffened, mouth tightening. Conor had arranged the bedrooms? But, knowing Conor, that would mean——

'Are you telling me,' Eleanor said tightly, mouth furious, 'that Conor Slade has organised the sleeping arrangements?'

'Well, as director, he has a moral duty to see that work can go ahead as smoothly and quickly as——'

'This is outrageous!' said Eleanor.

'I'm so sorry,' said Georgina, icily polite, 'but you must see his position. You're not employed on this film, Eleanor. You would only get in the way if you slept on the first floor.' She extended a ringed hand in the direction of the corridor. 'Now, please follow me!'

There was a tense silence. For a moment Diana thought her guardian would argue the case, put her foot down, cause an angry scene.

Then Eleanor swept out of the bedroom, her face glacial.

The door closed.

Incredible, she thought, amazed that Eleanor had given up so easily. Normally she would insist on being close to Diana. Was it because of Conor? Eleanor had never liked him...

But what a beautiful room! she thought, distracted as she stared in delight at the white-laced four-poster. The sun shafted in gold from the open balcony doors, burning her head and illuminating the ivory-gold Persian rug on the oak floor.

A key turned in a lock, and she turned, frowning. It was the connecting door. The handle was turning and Diana knew before it opened that it was Conor.

'Well,' he drawled, lounging in the open doorway, 'that went rather well, didn't it?'

Diana was breathless, staring at him, struggling to conceal the immediate and very powerful impact he always had on her. The open-necked white shirt and immaculate grey trousers made him look devastatingly French, every inch a casually wealthy count, at home in his skin in the magnificent château. Only the fierce blue blaze of his eyes belied his Celtic blood, and the scar on his tough cheekbone emphasised the danger of him, the terrible danger...

'You were listening!' Diana accused tightly. 'Listening at the door!'

'Not at all,' he returned, raising dark brows, 'I was lounging on my balcony drinking cold beer: your balcony doors are open, in case you hadn't noticed. Every word just sailed straight out to me.' He laughed, blue eyes rakishly amused. 'I expected it to take about ten minutes to convince Eleanor she wasn't going to be sleeping anywhere near you!'

'And how long did it take?' Diana asked resentfully.

'Two minutes forty-five seconds.'

Diana shrugged. 'Georgina was...persuasive.'

'Georgina was formidable,' Conor drawled, 'as I instructed her to be.'

'Then you are behind this?' she said angrily. 'And you deliberately took the connecting room!'

'I want to be close at hand,' he said under his breath, 'for when those barriers come crashing down.'

'They're not going to come crashing down!' she said furiously, hating him. 'This isn't the siege of Orleans!'

'And you're no Saint Joan!' he drawled, eyes mocking.

Her face ran with angry colour. She counted to ten, refusing to have an argument with him, particularly not in this very dangerous bedroom. 'This is a lovely room,' she said with an attempt at courtesy. 'Thank you.'

'Lovely manners,' he said. 'Very Garden Party.'

Her eyes flashed. 'Well, what do you expect me to say? I don't want to have this conversation with you and you know it!'

'No,' he said flatly, 'you'd much rather have a horizontal conversation on the bed with me!'

Outrage made her catch her breath, eyes furious. 'Will you stop this?'

'You know the answer to that,' he said under his breath.

She trembled at the obsessive, burning expression in his eyes. 'You shouldn't have put me in here! Not right next to you!'

'Why not?' he said coolly, hands thrust in grey trouser pockets.

'You know why!'

His eyes burnt on her. 'I'm afraid not. You'll have to say it out loud!'

'Because you know very well you're going to try and——' She had to say it, and her voice roughened with angry emotion as she forced it out '—try and seduce me!'

'Night after night,' he said thickly.

Diana shuddered. 'It'll never happen! Never!'

'Never... I'm always wary of that particular word,' drawled Conor, dark and dangerous in the doorway. 'It has a tendency to rebound on one.'

'Not this time! Not with me!'

'No?' he drawled, pushing away from the doorway, walking coolly towards her. 'Care to make a bet on that?'

Her body leapt in response as he moved towards her. She could barely breathe, staring at him and saying thickly, 'You shouldn't be in here! You shouldn't have done this...shouldn't have deliberately thrown us together like this!'

'Why not?' he said tightly, towering over her now in front of that gold and ivory bed. 'What are you scared of? Me—or yourself?'

'Don't be absurd!' she said, dragging her eyes from his hard, handsome face. 'Why should I be scared?'

His hand shot out, caught her chin, thrust her head up to face him. 'Because you want me!' he said tightly. 'And I'm going to make you admit it!'

'You're wasting your time!' she denied furiously, her eyes flashing.

'That's my look-out,' he said, 'and, until I give you notice otherwise, you will remain in this bedroom, next to mine!'

'Why are you doing this?'

'Because I'm running this show, Diana,' he told her under his breath, 'and what I say goes.'

She studied his jagged scar, then his eyes, and her mouth trembled as she realised how completely she was now in his power. Well, she wouldn't submit to it—not without a fight!

'I can play emperor,' Conor said softly, 'crack the whip, demand anything...indulge all my whims.' His eyes rested on her mouth. 'You're one of my whims, Diana. And you're unfortunate enough to find yourself in my power. And for the duration of this film...' his eyes scrutinised her angry face '...I want to see you play Cleopatra to my Caesar!'

'You can't force me to do anything!' she said with fierce determination not to give in. 'Not a thing!'

'No,' he agreed coolly, 'but I can make life damned near unliveable if you refuse to indulge me.'

Her eyes widened and she said thickly, 'You can't mean it, Conor! It would be unforgivable of you to...to demand sexual favours under these circumstances!'

'I'm not demanding them,' he said, mouth hard, 'I'm just going to landslide you into bed!'

'What's the difference?'

'The difference, my love,' he said hoarsely, 'is that you'll welcome it, when it finally happens! You'll kiss me back and push your fingers through my hair and tear me to pieces every bit as passionately as I tear you!' He drew a shaking breath, his eyes violent as he went on, 'I won't have it any other way, Diana!'

'Why not?' she demanded.

'Because it's all or nothing with me!' he said bitingly. 'It always has been, and you know it!'

She was trembling, breathing erratically, and she couldn't bring herself to reply to him, couldn't think of a single thing to say in self-defence. What an intolerable situation! Stuck here in this château with Conor Slade sleeping in the next room! How on earth would she survive this fortnight?

The telephone in Conor's room began to ring. Relief flooded Diana, almost making her legs weak.

Conor's mouth tightened. 'Damn!' He stepped back from her, moving towards the door. 'Remember our date tonight, Diana. We're dining out in town.'

'I haven't forgotten,' she said defiantly. 'I never forget emotional blackmail!' and she lifted her head proudly, though she kept one hand resting on the edge of the bed to steady herself.

'Good.' Conor was in the doorway, watching her. 'I'll knock for you at seven-thirty. Be ready!'

The door closed behind him and Diana sank on to the bed, trembling.

How on earth was she going to survive?

At seven-thirty she was dressed and ready after a scented bath. Her pink silk strapless dress was complemented by long pink silk evening gloves that gave an eroticism to her bare shoulders echoed by the thick diamond choker encircling her throat.

Not too sexy, she told herself, eyes darting over the outfit. The pink colour gave it an innocence which was echoed by the silk swathe of her blonde hair, and no one could have pointed a finger and accused her of blatant sensuality.

The sun was gleaming gold on the Loire Valley as she stood nervously at her balcony, looking out over the land of the château. The landscaped gardens were indeed magnificent. Statues and fountains and carved hedges... but beyond lay the real land mass, and it was that which drew her eyes, drew them inexorably to the wild bleached acres with thickly clustered trees bordering a cool lake, a small stream... horses grazing in a far field, a well baking in the heat and a large round dungeon at the far end of the land.

Birds were still singing, and crickets chirping when Conor rapped hard three times on her bedroom door.

Drawing a deep breath and refusing to be intimidated, she walked to answer it.

'My love,' he said, blue eyes blazing over her, resting on her mouth, her breasts, her slender waist. 'You look ravishing.'

'Thank you,' she said with a cool flick of her long lashes; although her heart leapt at the sight of him, leapt with that forbidden excitement at his devastating formality in that white evening jacket, black tie against white shirt and black evening trousers, she did not tell him how devastatingly attractive she found him . . . and how exciting was the combination of his harsh, jagged face with that civilised formality.

'Does Eleanor know?' Conor asked as they walked down the marble staircase, a warm breeze in their hair.

'That we're having dinner?' Diana shot him a quick frowning glance. 'No, of course not!'

He laughed softly. 'Hmm! And what excuse did you give her for not dining with her tonight?'

'I didn't give an excuse!' she said angrily. 'I told her the truth; that I had a headache after the drive from Paris.'

'A headache?' he said, black brows lifting. 'You seem fine to me.'

She gave a casual shrug. 'I took some aspirin. My headache wore off an hour ago.'

He laughed under his breath. 'Is there any point in saying that you're lying? And that we both know it?'

'Very little,' she said tightly, hating him, because of course the truth was that she had not had a headache at all, but had bridled angrily at his implication that she should have to give excuses to her guardian.

They walked out on to the steps of the château, down to the dusty pebble-strewn drive and towards a long steel-blue Citroën. The sun was gold, still warm, and the sky seemed infinite.

'Did she kick up a fuss?' Conor asked, black brows frowning.

'Eleanor? No,' Diana shook her blonde head, 'she had a headache herself.'

Conor opened the Citroën door, and his blue eyes flashed obsessively over Diana's body, over her bare shoulders and the blonde hair shimmering down her slender back, pink silk dress complementing her creamy skin and large blue eyes.

He got in behind the steering-wheel, and Diana's eyes slid sideways to stare at his long muscular legs. He was so tall, so dynamic, so very disturbing...

They drove away in a cloud of bleached dust, out through the wrought-iron gates and into the heart of France... Long straight roads lined with long straight trees, and the sun-baked land spreading out endlessly around them.

The town of le Lude was dominated by a large grey château. Conor drove the Citroën over the town's bridge, across the Loire herself, as the sun sank red-gold behind the distant trees along the banks.

People were everywhere, walking lazily in bright summer clothes, children holding balloons, youths drinking beer as they leant against their motorcycles, people eating out in the town's restaurant square, beneath rows of bright-leaved trees.

Conor parked, and they walked across the latticed bridge to the restaurant. It was obviously expensive. A bright scarlet canopy fluttered in the warm breeze, emblazoned with the legend: Roi de Soleil.

Diana's entrance caused something of a stir, and Conor was coolly amused as waiters fluttered about, admiring glances riveted on Diana, fighting each other for the privilege of handing her a menu and getting her a drink.

'What a little star you are!' Conor drawled, leaning back in his seat and watching her from beneath those hooded eyelids. 'You don't actually enjoy it very much though, do you?'

Diana flushed, looking up. 'I...I find it rather embarrassing sometimes.'

His eyes were ruthlessly shrewd. 'You feel a fraud.'

'Yes...' She looked down at her menu.

'As though it's not really you who's so famous?'

Diana gave a tense smile and said, 'I think I'll have the melon.'

'But it's not you who's famous, is it, Diana?' His eyes were hard. 'It's some blonde bombshell in pink. A creature of fantasy and imagination.'

Diana fingered the menu, deliberately not looking at him. 'We've been through all this, Conor! Back in London when you first——'

'How do you feel when you go to sleep at night?' he cut in, eyes hard. 'Is that the only time you feel real, Diana?'

There was a little silence.

'Is this amateur psychology night, Conor?' Diana asked in a brittle, tense voice.

The hard mouth was unsmiling. 'Yes. Why? Does it disturb you?'

'No,' she lied angrily, looking down, 'and I think I'll definitely have the melon.'

Conor laughed softly, watching her, and at that moment the waiter swept up to take their order. Diana ordered the melon, of course, followed by grilled lobster with salad. Her calorific intake each day was ruthlessly minimal, and while filming was in progress it was essential that she stuck to it.

The waiter poured the chilled Pouilly-Fuissé.

'Why did you insist I dine with you tonight, Conor?' Diana asked when they were alone.

He frowned and drawled, 'Why do you think?'

'Well,' she said carefully, 'you say you want revenge: but a civilised candle-lit dinner doesn't seem very vengeful...'

Conor smiled coolly. 'I once saw a tiger in India catch a gazelle, wound it, and then play with it for about an hour before he killed it.'

Diana stared, her heart thudding.

'We all play games, don't we, Diana? Sometimes those games can be deadly. Sometimes...' his eyes gleamed hard and ruthless '...well, they can just be so exciting you can't stop yourself playing them.'

'And,' her voice was thick with tension, 'am I a game to you, Conor? A gazelle to toy with until you deliver the final blow?'

'Let's just say I'm the predator and you're the prey.'

She drew a shaky breath. 'And if I ask you a serious question, would you answer it?'

'Try me,' he said, mouth hard.

'Are you——' she could barely say it '—are you trying to destroy me? I mean—is that what this is all about?'

He studied her through heavy lids. 'How could I attempt to destroy you? You're my life, my love, my hatred...my nemesis!' The blue eyes moved obsessively over her, seeing the shiver of fear and excitement that went through her body. 'I'd like to destroy you sometimes, Diana. Sometimes I feel capable of it. But I know I'd only be torturing myself if I did. In the long run...I need you. For good or bad; I need to know you're around. Regardless of how you behave towards me. Just watching you shiver as you did a moment ago is reward enough to me for—as you put it—torturing you.'

Diana stared at him, her heart pounding as his words sank into her fevered mind. The darkness that ran between them was growing, and it was electrifying. She could look into his eyes and see heaven and hell, both mixed into two dark whirlpools of emotion that threatened to engulf her and claim her forever.

'Now,' said Conor deeply, watching her with narrowed eyes, 'answer me a question—what did you do the day after we got married?'

'The day after we got married?' She struggled to look indifferent. 'I...I went back to England.'

'Now ask me what I did,' he said under his breath.

She sensed his anger suddenly, and her voice was husky as she said, 'Conor, don't start this ag——'

'All right!' he said with a cynical laugh. 'I'll tell you! I made love to you, got dressed, drove into the village to get some milk——'

'Conor, please!'

'And when I came back,' he said tightly, mouth hard, 'I found a hastily scrawled note on the kitchen table saying: "Our marriage was a terrible mistake. I'm sorry. Goodbye."'

Diana closed her eyes in silence.

'So I knocked myself out with a bottle of Scotch,' he went on softly, 'hated you, wanted to kill you, vowed to forget you. Then I woke up the next day in my clothes on the couch and hated myself.' He gave a harsh laugh. 'Too much hatred for one day, Diana! Too damned much!'

'I didn't want you to hate me, Conor, I really——'

'I cleaned myself up,' he said bitingly, 'I left the cottage, and I flew back to England to find you and demand an explanation. But I didn't find you: instead I found Eleanor.'

'Eleanor?' She stared at him for a second, then said, 'What do you mean—you "found Eleanor"?'

'She was riding on the estate,' Conor said flatly. 'She saw my car before I was even halfway up the drive. Galloped over to me, blocked my path, told me in no uncertain terms that you hated me... and that you would die rather than let me into the house.'

'But I...' Diana was bewildered, confused '...I didn't even know you'd tried to see me!'

Conor studied her in silence for a moment. One long finger ran over his hard mouth. 'Really, Diana?' he drawled sardonically. 'You mean to say she didn't tell you?'

She stared at him in silence for a long time. The restaurant was getting crowded now. More people were arriving, and outside one could dimly perceive a lot of people on the streets.

'How very remiss of Eleanor,' drawled Conor, raising one dark brow. 'Imagine forgetting to tell you.' He drank a little more wine. 'Imagine that!'

Diana just sat where she was, staring at him and thinking, I can't believe it! Surely Eleanor would have told me if Conor had followed me? But it all seemed so long ago, and she couldn't see where truth ended and revenge began.

'So then,' Conor continued, 'I went off and got smashed out of my head again. I wasn't feeling too good. A little massacred—just around the edges.'

'Conor, you must stop this!' she whispered, palms damp as she pushed her half-eaten melon away, feeling sick.

'But I wasn't going to give up!' he drawled under his breath. 'Not me! Not Conor Slade...army hero, ex-SAS, a tough guy from way back! So I came back the next day, and then the next——'

'No!' Diana's heart was thudding with panic. 'No, I won't believe it!'

'But Eleanor had left instructions at the gate that I wasn't to be let through.' He laughed hoarsely, blue eyes blazing. 'I remember seeing the funny side, of course, because that's just what my father did when I left the SAS to run off and marry you.'

Diana's eyes were suddenly motionless. 'Yes, I remember you told me...he was so cruel.'

'Cruel?' Conor studied her, eyes hard. 'Yes, he was. But not as cruel as the woman who ran off and left that apology for a letter behind!'

Her eyes flashed and she said defensively, 'It was a perfectly reasonable letter!'

'It was a kick in the teeth and you know it!'

She flushed hotly, eyes darting. 'I didn't have time to make it any more detailed than——'

'You couldn't be bothered!'

'That's not true!'

He gave an angry laugh. 'Any minute now you'll be getting back on the QE2 and sailing off around the world again, won't you? Anything to run away from the truth, Diana! Anything at all!'

'I went on the QE2 to forget!' she said angrily. 'Don't you understand that?'

His mouth hardened. 'To forget me?'

'Who else?' Her eyes shone with tears of anger and frustration, and she bit her lip, suddenly appalled as she realised there were tears trying to sting the back of her eyes.

'I see...' Conor said under his breath. 'So you didn't just walk out and never give me another thought?'

'Of course not!' she said at once, looking up, then realised she had betrayed herself and was at once in a terrible rush to counterbalance her own words. 'We were married...how could I have forgotten just like that...how could any woman...?'

'You loved me!' he said quietly.

'No!' she denied at once. 'I—I was just very young and I'd made a terrible mistake. It was wonderful of Eleanor to intervene like that, to take me on a world cruise to help me forget and——'

'Wonderful!' he said tightly. 'I could kill her for it!'

'Conor, must you be so violent about——?'

'Yes!' he said angrily, and his hand bit into her wrist across the table. 'Yes, I damned well must be! I was deprived of my wife—of the woman I loved!'

'You didn't love me!' she burst out fiercely. 'You just wanted to make love to me and——'

The waiter appeared and Diana froze, looking away to hide her tears and trying very hard to buckle her emotions down, out of sight, hating Conor for having whirled them up again, just as he always had, just as he always would. She could remember how passionate and intense their love had been, and she knew she could not possibly allow it to sweep her up again. Not into that whirlwind. Not into that fiery madness, the vortex of love, the twin pillars of pleasure and pain.

Keep your cool! she told herself determinedly. Just have dinner with him, work with him, don't get involved, however much those blue eyes and that hard mouth and that strong, hard, sexy body induce you to lose your head.

But, as she looked down at the lobster, and it peered back with a baleful eye, she knew she would not be able to eat much of it. Even the crisp green salad served with it did not interest her now. Her appetite was shot to pieces.

They ate with indifference. Their eyes clashed constantly across the table, and every time they did Diana's heart raced.

'Do you want coffee?' Conor asked as their plates were eventually cleared and night had set in outside the pretty latticed windows of the restaurant. 'A liqueur?'

She shook her blonde head. 'I'd rather just go.'

The blue eyes gleamed mockingly. 'Home to bed? Very well!' He signalled for the bill with one long finger.

'I didn't mean it like that!' Diana said at once, heart banging.

'No,' he said flatly, dropping a gold American Express card on the table and taking a silver pen from his inside jacket pocket, 'but I did. And we do have a connecting door. For moments when passion becomes quite intolerable...'

'Your passion is always intolerable!' she said fiercely, hating him as he bent his dark head to sign the bill.

'Is it?' His eyes flicked like lasers to hers. 'How very encouraging.'

They left the restaurant at nine-thirty. The sky was a dark blue, dotted with stars, and the moon shone down over the dark waters of the Loire.

'Why are there so many people about?' Diana asked with a frown as people in bright summer clothes milled around, balloons and crêpes and beer in assorted hands.

'Some sort of local celebration, I expect,' Conor said with a broad shrug.

They walked across the latticed bridge over the Loire.

'Hang on a minute,' Conor said suddenly, stopping and turning to her with a dark frown. 'What's the date?'

'July the fourteenth.'

There was a brief silence.

'Of course!' they said in sudden chorus. 'It's——'

An ear-shattering explosion rent the air.

Their eyes snapped wide open as they stared at each other in black, remembered terror, and, as Diana moved towards him with a gasp of shock, so he moved towards her, and they were both catapulted into the past...

Diana Sullivan had black hair when she was seventeen. Long straight black hair right down to her waist, blazing blue eyes, a generous smile and a quick, intelligent mind.

When she arrived home from boarding-school that hot, heady July, she found Eleanor in a dither over what to do for the summer.

'It's your Uncle Claudius,' Eleanor told her as the maid took Diana's cases up to her room. 'He's had a heart attack. I must go to him at once.'

'Yes, of course,' Diana said immediately, appalled and concerned over her only other living relative. 'Poor Uncle Claudius! I hope he survives until we get to New York...'

'We?' Eleanor's face stiffened. 'I'm sorry, Diana. You obviously misunderstand.'

Diana's eyes dulled as she said slowly, 'You mean you don't want me to——?'

'It's not a case of wanting, Diana.' Eleanor was icily formal. 'It's simply a question of good manners.'

Diana nodded, falling silent.

'I'm afraid Claudius had the same opinion of your mother as I did,' Eleanor said flatly. 'As all of us did. How could we help but despise her? Such wanton behaviour. Such a destructive woman. Nothing good ever came of her, you know. But none of us can forget...'

'But Mama,' Diana said, 'surely Uncle Claudius will——'

'No!' Eleanor said icily. 'You'll remind him too much of her—just as you remind me. Every day you grow more like her. Well, I won't have you walking in, the image of Allannah, and ruining my brother's last moments.'

So Diana went to London, to stay with her schoolfriend, Sophie Blake and her parents, while Eleanor flew to New York.

Mr and Mrs Blake lived in an elegant Georgian house in a leafy London square, five minutes' walk from Harrods. From the minute Diana arrived, she was left to fend for herself. Sophie had a boyfriend, and spent every possible moment with him. Mr and Mrs Blake were socialites, and rarely at home. Diana knew nobody in London, and therefore spent much of her time alone, either in the house or sightseeing, going to theatres, shopping.

On bright Sunday afternoon Diana was walking through Knightsbridge past the army barracks when a small black car roared down the street behind her, screeched to a halt in front of her at the gates of the

barracks and the driver started blaring his horn, fierce
blue eyes blazing as he realised the guard on gate duty
was on the phone to someone.

Diana paused, staring into the open window of the
car as the man looked up at her, furious, then suddenly
opened the door and leapt out of the car.

Breathless, Diana stood rooted to the spot, watching
as the dynamic man in black raced to the closed gates
and shouted bitingly, 'Get off the phone and get these
damned gates open!'

The guard slammed the phone down, scarlet in the
face.

The man in black turned to race back into his car, but
Diana was standing motionless, directly in his way. For
a split second their eyes met and held in a moment of
sudden terrifying understanding.

Then the bomb went off and the air vibrated with
sound.

Everything went into slow motion. The man flung
himself towards her, but it was as though gravity had
ceased to exist, and the noise reverberating in her ears
was that of dark chaos as she fell backwards on to the
pavement, and he fell with her.

Sound returned with unexpected violence as windows
blew outwards and she looked up into the man's hard
face just in time to hear his rough gasp as he covered
her face with strong brown hands just before the glass
finally hit them. It showered everywhere. It was all she
could hear as she lay beneath him, her face covered by
his hands, and heard that glass shattering all around
them, tiny shards in her arms and legs and hair...but
not on her face.

There was a second's absolute silence.

Then people were screaming and a siren began to wail
inside the barracks. The strong brown hands left her face.

'Oh, my God!' Diana whispered as she saw the lethal
shard of glass embedded in his hard cheek. Blood ran
from the wound and splattered on to her white blouse.

'Are you hurt?' the man asked harshly, getting to his
feet. 'Can you walk?'

'Yes...!' Diana was standing, her hand in his as she stared around, dazed at the chaos. 'Was it a bomb?'

'The Brastaka Terrorist Group planted it. We had a sixty-second warning!' His eyes were furious. 'Sixty seconds! I was in the next street——' He broke off as cries from the rubble caught their attention. 'I must help!' he said under his breath, and turned to Diana, saying deeply, 'Wait here for the ambulances. You need medical attention.'

Diana watched him run to the still-closed gates and climb them with the effortless skill of a professional, dropping down the other side in a perfectly executed roll before leaping straight up again to run to the wounded and the dying.

Sirens sounded in the distance, and, as the ambulances, police cars and fire engines rolled up, Diana heard the distant whirr of a helicopter as the casualties began to be counted.

The hospital didn't keep her long. She had to lie in her lingerie behind a screen while a nurse painstakingly pulled every piece of glass from her body. Hot sweet tea was then served to all minor casualties, and, when Diana had finished hers, she offered her assistance to the nurses who were absolutely frantic in their efforts to cope with the sudden influx of casualties.

She found out that no one had been killed. What luck! Of course, many people were injured, but mainly by falling glass. The sixty-second warning had saved countless lives.

Someone gave her the job of making tea for the shock and minor-injury victims and keeping them calm while she did it. She worked diligently, her smooth oval face serious and deeply concerned as she handed round tea and blankets.

At seven o'clock the man in black came to the hospital. He had finally allowed himself to be brought in for medical attention.

He stopped in the corridor, seeing her as she made more tea in the kitchens.

'Hi,' he said, motionless as he stared at her.

'Come along, Mr Slade,' said the nurse, tugging at his sleeve.

He moved forwards, ignoring her, and stood framed in the doorway, blue eyes fixed intently on Diana. 'Are you a nurse?' he asked.

'No,' Diana said simply, blood still on her blouse from his injury. 'I'm just helping out.'

He nodded, unsmiling. 'What's your name?'

'Diana,' she said, her face calm. 'Diana Sullivan.'

'Come along, Mr Slade!' the nurse said irritably. 'We haven't got time to spare!'

He ignored her, his eyes fixed on Diana. 'Will you still be here when I get out? I shouldn't be more than twenty minutes.'

Her heart skipped several beats but she said coolly, 'Yes, of course,' and then, in a further attempt to be light-hearted, 'Looks to me as though you will need three stitches.'

He merely nodded, still unsmiling, turned on his heel and followed the nurse back down the corridor, leaving Diana in the kitchen staring into space and seeing nothing but those blazing, intense, passionate blue eyes and the jagged scar above that tough mouth.

When he came back, he had three stitches in his cheek. 'You were right,' he drawled with a faint smile. 'I had three.'

Diana smiled back. 'A lucky guess.'

'Which none the less deserves a prize.' He studied her mouth, the blood on her blouse, and then looked back into her eyes. 'Are you finished here? Would you like to have a light supper somewhere with me?'

Breathless, she struggled to keep a composed expression, saying coolly, 'Yes...thank you...'

They had dinner at a French bistro just around the corner, and, by the end of the evening, Diana knew she was in love with the dark, dynamic Conor Slade. When he stopped his car outside the house and looked at her in the darkness she knew he was going to kiss her, and she met his hard mouth with as much composure as she could, though her heart was banging and her breathing erratic.

Nothing could have prepared her for that kiss. Although it began with cool control, and Conor held her gently for the first few minutes, he must have heard her heart banging with excitement because he suddenly made a rough sound of pleasure under his breath and the next moment she was gasping under the onslaught of a hard, driving kiss, and as she slid back against her seat with a breathless moan of surrender so his kiss became more demanding and the strong hands that framed her face bit into her skin with a force that insisted she think ahead in a split second and know that if this man ever made love to her fully it would be a devastating, wildly exciting experience.

He had dragged his mouth from hers, breathing harshly, and as he'd stared down at her and said thickly, 'I want to see you again!' she had known that was it: she was in love and so was he and it was the love of their lives...

Fireworks exploded in the dark sky in the present. Diana and Conor were in each other's arms, staring in that few seconds of shared recall, and, as the colours blazed across the sky, reflecting like scattered jewels on the Loire, the memory faded and they were both slammed back into the present...

'Bastille Day!' Conor said thickly, staring at her. 'The fourteenth of July!'

'Of course!' Diana replied, staring back at him. 'How could we have forgotten?'

There was a long, tense silence.

'Well...' Diana could not hold his gaze any longer and tried to move away, saying huskily, 'How silly of us to think it was a...a...'

'A bomb,' he said deeply, watching her. 'Old habits die hard.'

She gave a pained laugh and felt tears sting her eyes. 'You're not in the SAS now, Conor! You're a film director and we both have to work tomorrow.'

'You prefer to forget, do you?' he demanded under his breath, his hands tightening on her waist. 'You prefer to just brush it all aside?'

'What else can I do?' she asked huskily, unable to look him in the face. 'It was so long ago...'

'It was yesterday and you know it!' he said fiercely. 'This is the first time we've been able to be together for six years, Diana, and it's all still there—every bit as devastating as it was when we met!'

'I don't want to talk about it!' she said, trying to pull away.

'No,' he said tightly, eyes hating her, 'but you think about it—don't you? Now that I'm back. Now that I'm beating down your defences one by one, smashing them all into oblivion and dragging you back into the land of the living!'

'I don't think about it!' she denied hoarsely, closing her eyes. 'I never, never think about it!'

'Like hell!' he said thickly, mouth hard. 'Like hell, Diana!'

She flinched, breaking away from him, her face white, and when he simply let her go she almost stopped and turned to him in surprise, but she realised at the last minute how silly she would look if she did, so she faltered but did not look, and a second later she was running across that latticed bridge and back to the car.

When Conor reached the car, his eyes were hard and angry, but he said nothing as he opened her door and watched her slide in. Diana did not meet his blue eyes. She tensed as the door slammed shut and he strode round to the driver's side, getting in and slamming his door angrily.

The car engine flared. He drove away, not looking at her and not speaking. Diana looked out of the windows at the darkness, and insects danced in the headlights as they roared through the countryside, finally turning into the drive of the château and speeding up it to the entrance.

Conor plunged out the lights. Diana was rigid with tension. Those glittering blue eyes flicked towards her in the darkness.

'You think I'm going to make love to you, don't you?' he asked tightly and she could feel his hatred.

'I . . . I think you're going to try!' she bit out, hating him back. 'And I know I'm going to fight if you do!'

His mouth hardened and he said bitingly under his breath, 'I'd rather cut off my hands and bleed to death than ever make love to you again, you bitch!'

Diana flinched, fumbling for the door-handle and stumbling out of the car. She found herself running in through the open doors of the château, aware that Conor had not even got out of the car.

The tears were hot and swiftly falling by the time she got to her room, whirled in blindly and locked the door behind her. Sinking down on the floor, she wept, her hands at her wet face, and the inner conflict truly began . . .

She knew instinctively that chaos was now only a footstep away and she was horrified to realise that a part of her, a small part of her long since buried, was suddenly crying out for that chaos to begin, as though only destruction could bring salvation.

'No!' Diana whispered, horrified at her own thoughts, and the beautiful bedroom was silent as she whispered again, fiercely, 'No, I don't want it!'

Yes! whispered the voice inside her, like Lucifer in the wilderness. Yes, you do!

Appalled, Diana's tears stopped at once, and she got to her feet, white and obsessive as she walked slowly to the bed and sank down on it, blonde hair sliding like corn-silk over her bare shoulders, the pink dress gleaming against her creamy skin.

She saw herself in the mirror.

She saw herself at seventeen, with long black hair and blood on her blouse and chaos all around her as she stared into Conor Slade's blazing eyes and fell in love.

Terrified, she quickly shut her eyes to try and blot it all out, but there was no silencing that small, long-forgotten voice inside her now that Conor had blasted it into life again.

The inner conflict had suddenly become full-scale war...

CHAPTER FOUR

WHEN Diana woke the next morning, she felt as though something essential had changed within her. No matter how much she told herself that everything was the same as it had been before her twenty-fourth birthday, she knew it wasn't.

Conor Slade had blasted his way back into her life with the same force with which he had first appeared, and the effect of his reappearance was now becoming that of a jagged stone thrown into a still lake, causing ripples to spread out in a wide circle from the very centre of herself.

He's getting to me, she realised, and was furious.

Quickly, she showered in the exquisite antique-style bathroom. Wrapping a fluffy blue bath-towel around herself, she padded into the bedroom again, her hair wet, her body clean and dripping, and as she walked across the room she heard a noise from the bedroom next door.

Diana froze, staring at the connecting door. A key turned in the lock. The handle began to twist.

'Don't come in, Conor!' Diana burst out, horribly aware of her nudity beneath the blue bath-towel.

But he pushed back the door and his powerful body was framed in the doorway. For a long moment their eyes met and held. He looked superb in a white shirt and black trousers, his black hair damp from a shower, his blue eyes blazing from that tanned, clean-shaven face.

'Please,' Diana said huskily, heart thumping like mad, 'please don't come in. Not now. Not after last night. Not——'

'I'll enter your bedroom as I please,' Conor said tightly, hands thrusting into the pockets of his black trousers. 'I'm your husband. I have the right to——'

'We're divorced!' she reminded him hotly. 'How many times must I remind you?'

'After last night?' he said under his breath. 'Don't tell me you didn't remember it all last night, Diana, because I don't believe it! Not for one second! You relived it all with me when those damned fireworks went off! I saw it in your face! Yet you ran away from the memory—just as you ran from our marriage!'

'Conor, for God's sake!'

Rage flared in his eyes and he strode towards her suddenly, catching her bare shoulders in biting hands. 'I came to make sure we could work together today without this kind of emotional battlefield flaring up between us on set. But it's impossible, isn't it?' He stared: obsessive, passionate, determined; and his voice said thickly, 'You can't pretend indifference to me any more than I can to you.'

'Why do you think I didn't want to work with you in the first place?' she muttered, clutching the towel at her bare breasts. 'Why do you think I keep running from you?'

His blue gaze fell to her trembling mouth. 'Because you want me as much as I want you! There's always been a chemical explosion between us!' His voice deepened and he murmured, 'Don't you know it yet?'

'But we have to work together... we have to——'

'Don't talk about work now,' he cut in, eyes sliding down to the breasts which rose and fell beneath the blue towel. 'Not when I'm here alone with you and you look like this...' He stared down at her quivering body. 'You're so lovely... My God, Diana, how do you inflame me so damned fast?'

His dark head swooped, but before his hard mouth could possess hers the telephone shrilled into life.

'Damn them!' Conor swore hoarsely, lifting his head but staring at her mouth still. 'How do they manage to be so inopportune?'

'I must answer it,' Diana said, shaking from head to foot.

His mouth hardened and he gave a brief nod, stepping back and releasing her. Diana moved towards the telephone shakily, overwhelmingly aware of his hot blue gaze on her slim bare legs and slim bare shoulders and the pulse that beat achingly at her throat.

'Diana Sullivan,' she said huskily into the receiver.

The telephone in Conor's bedroom began to ring.

'Damn!' Conor bit out, turning and striding back into his room.

'Your wake-up call, Miss Sullivan!' said the production secretary.

'Thank you,' Diana said and quickly replaced the receiver, shut the connecting door between her room and Conor's, ran to the wardrobe, selected a pale blue cotton sun-dress to wear, grabbed some filmy lingerie, and raced into the bathroom, locking the door behind her to dress.

If Conor came back into her room before going to work, he found it deserted. When Diana emerged from the bathroom dressed in the pale blue sun-dress, the room was empty.

After breakfast, Georgina took Diana to the drawing-room to meet her 'absolute poppet' of a drama coach.

'Geoff, darling!' Georgina said with a flourish as she guided Diana into the high-ceilinged, pale lemon room. 'I want you to meet your new protégée—Diana Sullivan.'

The man standing by the french windows turned, his blond hair gleaming in the sun, and Diana was surprised to see that Georgina had not been teasing her: Geoff really was very attractive. He was blond, handsome and well-dressed, and there was tremendous charm in his smile, and in his pale blue eyes.

'Miss Sullivan!' he said, walking towards her in a grey suit and open-necked white shirt. 'Wonderful to meet you, and to be working with you. I'm quite a fan...seen all your films!'

'I've only made seven,' Diana laughed, looking at him and being astonished again by his looks. Most of her drama coaches had been serious, studious types hidden by beards and Jean-Paul-Sartre-type clothes; dark intellectuals who treated her with disdain.

'Geoff is quite well known himself,' said Georgina. 'Surely you've heard of him?'

Diana looked embarrassed and shook her head.

'Geoff Hastings?' Georgina prompted.

'Oh...!' Diana stared, the penny dropping, and said, 'My goodness, yes! I have heard of you! But——' she stared at his tanned skin and blue eyes and charming smile '—but I expected you to be a lot older!'

'I'm flattered,' Geoff said wryly, smiling.

'Well,' Georgina drifted away to the door, 'I'll leave you two to work...'

'Sit down, Miss Sullivan.' Geoff Hastings indicated a pale gold brocade chair, and Diana moved to it, sitting down, her blue dress elegant and sensuous on her slender body.

'We're doing the unicorn scene today, aren't we?' Diana asked him, noticing his eyes flickering over her legs and feeling rather ill at ease.

'Yes, yes...' Geoff quickly turned the pages of his script, sitting opposite her on the couch. 'But I'd like to take a look at a dialogue scene, if I may, and...'

They worked for two hours, then Geoff suggested a break. Diana was exhausted but exhilarated.

'Awfully efficient, aren't they?' Geoff said when the caterer had disappeared and they were relaxing with hot, refreshing cups of tea.

'Yes,' Diana said a little too sharply, 'nobody would dare be anything less under the rule of the great emperor!'

Geoff frowned, studying her. 'The who?'

'Oh...' Diana shrugged '...the emperor. Just—just a little joke about Mr Slade.'

'Ah...' Geoff narrowed his eyes at her. 'What do you think of him?'

Diana was tempted, but managed to hold her tongue. 'He's very good at taking control. Ex-army. Very disciplined.' She shrugged, trying to look unaffected. 'I'm sure he'll do a brilliant job.'

'Hmm.' Geoff's smile was wry. 'I asked what you thought of him.'

Diana lowered her lashes and said huskily, 'He's all right.'

Geoff nodded. 'In other words you don't like him.'

'I didn't say that!' she denied, looking up sharply.

'You didn't have to,' said Geoff.

Diana moistened her lips. 'I guess I just find his type rather alarming...' How could she possibly tell him why she really disliked Conor? Because he made her heart race and her blood throb and her whole body crackle with electricity... As Conor himself had said that morning, there had been a chemical reaction between them since the day they met, and time had only heightened it.

'Yes, I'm sure you do,' Geoff said with a frown, nodding as he studied her. 'You're much too feminine to be able to cope with a one-man war like Conor Slade!'

'A one-man war...' Diana said thickly, staring, her mouth dry.

'Well, he is, isn't he?'

Yes, she thought, her soul blazing with that blood-red sky over Connemara and the fierce passion of the man who had held her there, held her now, refused to let go...

Geoff sipped his tea, the sun pouring in through the french windows. 'I've worked on films with him before, you see. I've seen him in action ... everybody jumps and everybody respects him: but nobody loves the guy.'

'Do you think so?' Diana frowned, thinking of the people she had known who had loved Conor: loved him deeply and with such fierce loyalty. He was that kind of man. He inspired steadfast love: she couldn't believe Geoff Hastings was right about that.

'Oh, definitely!' Geoff was adamant. 'I can't think of anyone on our last picture, *The Derringer*, who really came away liking him.'

'Then why do you work with him?' Diana asked, puzzled.

Geoff laughed. 'Why do any of us work with anyone? We have to—it's as simple as that. And Slade does make good films. No question about it. Big box-office, a handful of awards... He's a good director with powerful connections.'

'Yes, he ousted Teddy Godwin for this. I mean—I'm not sure he actually ousted him, but he's directing and Godwin isn't, so...' She shrugged lightly.

'I'm sure you're right,' Geoff agreed at once. 'Slade's got the Coral family in his back pocket. I mean—Georgina adores him, old Jack Coral goes out on the town drinking whisky and rye with him...' He shrugged. 'They're thick as thieves.'

Diana suddenly thought: thick as thieves?

Slowly, she put her cup down, staring out at the sunlight through the french windows. If Conor was very friendly with both Jack and Georgina Coral—surely he would have mentioned his marriage to them by now?

Things started whirling into place. The sudden *fait accompli* of Conor as director. The way she'd been put in a bedroom next to Conor. The way Georgina kept taking Eleanor away and leaving her alone with Conor...

'I...I suppose Conor would tell Georgina everything?' she asked Geoff suddenly, looking back at him, and held her breath.

'Definitely.' Geoff nodded. 'As I said—thick as thieves. Anyway—shall we get back to work?'

Diana spent the rest of the morning working hard with him on her dialogue. But now she was beginning to believe it was possible Conor had told Georgina Coral about their earlier marriage, and that Georgina was manipulating her as much as Conor was.

The thought was unpalatable. She found it hard to concentrate and could barely look Georgina in the eye when they had lunch.

At three-thirty, Diana was called to board the coach. The scene was being shot on the edge of the Balzac forest, close to the lake. She had to be in her trailer for makeup and costume by four.

She saw Conor at once, of course.

At the edge of the forest, he stood tall and dark and authoritative, biting out orders to the crew, surrounded by cameras and cables and trucks with power supplies.

Her trailer was blue and silver, sitting at the far end of the field. Diana went in and read her script while the make-up artist pinned her hair back, scrubbed her face and began applying make-up with exceptional skill.

The film was a legend, set in another world, and was about the royal family of a mythical kingdom who were about to be destroyed by a witch who had control of their world and was marching on their castle with her own followers. The only way the royal family could save themselves was with white magic, and their only hope was the unicorn of Sarcaronne. It was the unicorn depicted in their family crest, and the legend ran that if the Sarcaronne family were ever in danger the unicorn from their crest would come to life and save them.

The scene they were about to shoot was where Princess Alara—Diana—first saw the unicorn at the edge of the royal forest at twilight.

At five o'clock, Diana stepped out of the trailer.

People stared as she walked past. The blue dress was richly embroidered, and the laced corset not only emphasised her tiny waist but also thrust her breasts into a cleavage of wild sensuality, accentuated by the innocence of her blue eyes. Her blonde hair was piled in sensual ringlets on top of her head, and jewels flashed at her throat.

The unicorn stood by the edge of the forest. The white horn rose, as in legend, from his forehead, his noble head lifted as the gold light of the dying sun flashed on his white flanks.

'Ah...' Conor turned as Diana approached '... Miss Sullivan!' His blue eyes flashed over her, resting with insolent appraisal on her breasts and tiny waist. 'I hope you read my direction comments in the script?'

'Of course.' Diana lifted her head, fighting her instinctive response to his presence. 'I've been rehearsing them all day with my coach.' She did not, of course, say anything about her conversation with Geoff, but as she looked at Conor her hostility showed in her eyes.

'Your eyes have gone very dark, my love,' Conor said under his breath, his own eyes narrowing with suspicion. 'Nothing wrong, I hope?'

Her eyes regarded him, anger in their depths, but she was silent.

'Good.' He gave a hard smile of satisfaction. 'I'll show you your places. They're marked with black gaffer tape, as always...' He moved around the field with her, commenting on her places as he did, then straightened and said, 'When you turn to see the unicorn at the edge of the forest, you simply catch your breath and stare.'

'Total disbelief,' she agreed, nodding.

'But then you hear your father's, the king's, voice in your mind saying, "If only that old legend were true! If only the unicorn of the family crest would come to life to save us from the witch!" And at that moment you realise it has happened, it's not a dream: the ancient magic of the Sarcaronne family has stirred in its long-forgotten grave.'

'So I move towards the unicorn slowly, and touch it before I ride it?'

'Yes. And think of me when you caress it,' Conor said softly, one long finger stroking her pale cheek. 'Think of me when you mount it and ride it across the land...'

Diana leaped away as though scalded. 'Please don't touch me like that publicly!'

'I'll do as I damned well please!' he said tightly, his hand shooting out to bite into her wrist.

'People are staring!' she said, face running with hot colour.

His mouth hardened. 'Let them stare!'

'But—do you want everyone to know what's happening between us?'

'It's not high on my list of priorities,' he said flatly, 'but if it puts my brand of possession on you it can't do any harm!'

She was appalled. 'Your brand of possession?'

'Yes,' he said, eyes narrowing, 'and if you object strenuously enough I'll kiss you thoroughly in front of all of them! Do I make myself clear?'

Bitterly, her eyes met his and warred rebelliously for a few seconds. But she could see he meant it. He really would kiss her in front of the whole cast and crew if she argued further.

'You make yourself very clear, Conor!' she said at last, angry submission in the set of her mouth.

'Good,' Conor drawled, eyes mocking. 'I'm glad to see you so obedient. Now get to your first place. I want to finish this scene some time this week!'

He turned on his heel and strode to the director's chair. Picking up the loudspeaker, he looked at Diana and commanded, 'Action!'

Diana ran into shot, breathless, and sank to the first black marker. Piece by piece, she followed every one of Conor's instructions to the letter. Her professionalism was not going to be destroyed by her passion.

The unicorn was released, and Diana looked up to see it stepping out of the trees, its horn piercing the gold sky. Slowly, she moved towards it, embraced its strong white neck.

'Mount it . . .' Conor's voice said deeply.

She kicked off her shoes, gripped the unicorn's mane, and hoisted herself on to its back. The blue-gold skirt rose up around her thighs, and she felt a thrill of excitement as she kicked the unicorn into a fast canter, rolling out across the gold-lit field.

Galloping now, the wind in her hair, she rode to the far edge of the field, beyond the cameras, and executed a perfect turn, riding back towards Conor, her face flushed and her eyes glittering with pleasure.

'How was that?' she called to him, for she knew it was perfect.

'Passable,' said Conor coolly.

Her mouth dropped open. 'Passable!'

'Yes.' His hard eyes dared her to argue. 'Get back to make-up and do it again.' He stood up. 'Five minutes, people!'

Gritting her teeth, Diana did as she was told. The whole scene was shot again from the beginning, and when it was over, Diana rode back to her director, sweat on her lovely face, and said breathlessly, 'Was that better?'

'No,' Conor drawled, watching her. 'Do it again.'

Anger prickled at her, but she clamped down on it, went back to her trailer, suffered the removal of sweat and dirt and the reapplication of make-up, struggling to be professional about it.

Truth was, she felt humiliated. And Conor knew it, damn him, as he made her ride that damned unicorn again and again. For the next two hours, she did nothing but catch the unicorn and ride him.

The light was dying fast, but still he made her ride. By eight o'clock, she had bruises and grazes on her hands from gripping that mane, but still he made her ride.

For the umpteenth time, Diana turned the unicorn and rode back to her director. 'How was that?' she asked, sweat-streaked. 'Can I stop now?'

'No,' Conor said. 'Do it again!'

'For God's sake!' Diana exploded hoarsely. 'I'm exhausted! So is the horse! So are the crew! The light's dying and——'

'And you'll damned well ride until I tell you to stop!'

Rage rose in her like a tidal wave and poured out, unstoppable. 'The hell I will!' She shook with it, eyes blazing. 'The hell I will!' A ripple ran through the crew. Diana leapt down from the horse, trembling. 'You can just demand anything you damned well please, Conor! You can sit up there and play emperor and demand that I do it all again, but you'll be wasting your breath, and cracking your whip to an empty stage, because nothing can make me do your bidding, nothing can make me do that scene again, and nothing can stop me walking off your stupid, stupid, *stupid* set!'

Storming across the bleached grass to her trailer, she banged the door open on its hinges, shouted, 'Damn him to hell!' and slammed the door so hard the trailer walls rattled.

'What?' Liza the redheaded make-up girl jumped out of her skin.

'I'd rather die,' Diana ranted hysterically, pacing the trailer, 'than ever work for that tyrant, that sadistic bully, that absolute——'

The trailer door banged open.

'Oh, Mr Slade,' began Liza, 'so nice to see——'

'Get out!' said Conor. 'I want to talk to Miss Sullivan alone!'

'Right-oh, sir!' Liza scurried to the door.

Conor slammed it behind her, blues eyes blazing. 'All right! What's got into you? Why did you throw that temper tantrum just——?'

'Temper tantrum?' She was incredulous. 'How dare you accuse me of throwing a temper tantrum? I just spent three hours doing that damned scene over and over again, and——'

'It's your job,' he said flatly. 'Just as it's my job to decide when I'm ready to stop shooting.'

'But that scene was perfect the first time!'

'Was it?' he said, dark brows lifting in cool contradiction. 'I don't think so, Diana. And I'm the overseer—remember? You can never be sure you're judging your own work correctly. Particularly when you're the actor. But a director...'

'Don't lie to me!' she said angrily. 'You made me do that scene over and over again, and you did it deliberately to annoy me!'

His hard mouth crooked in a sardonic smile. 'Well,' he drawled, 'I admit I pushed it a little close to the edge, but——'

'But nothing,' she said. 'You pushed it right over the edge and you know it!'

'I can see you've been pushed over the edge,' Conor said with a sudden narrowing of the eyes, and he moved towards her, studying her closely. 'I noticed a jumpiness when you first arrived on set but you said nothing was wrong. That was a lie—wasn't it?'

Diana lifted her head. 'It's our first scene together. I was nervous. What did you expect?'

He took her chin in his hand and pushed it up to look at him. 'That's not it,' he said flatly. 'If it was that simple, you would have reacted differently. You certainly wouldn't have thrown a prima donna tantrum and stormed off the——'

'It was not a prima donna tantrum!' she denied angrily, prickling at the suggestion of unprofessionalism.

'No?' Dark brows lifted coolly. 'You scream at your director, refuse to do another take and storm off the set hurling abuse left, right and centre. Forgive me, but that smacks of——'

'All right,' she said tightly, 'it was very... unprofessional of me. But you did provoke it, Conor, and you know it!'

'I know something provoked it,' he said, eyes narrowing, 'but I don't appear to be getting any answers from you, do I? Now: I'll ask you again. What happened before you arrived on set to make you react like this?'

Diana studied him for a long moment, holding her breath, hating him for being so clever. Then she pulled out of his grasp and averted her head, blonde hair shining as she said, 'All right! I—I was already upset by the time I got here. And it—it wasn't just because it was my first time working with you.'

'Then what?' He pushed his hands in his pockets, watching her closely.

She moistened her lips then turned to confront him with it. 'You told Georgina Coral about us. About our marriage.'

There was a silence.

'Didn't you, Conor? You told her everything.'

His mouth pursed and he drawled slowly, 'She knows we were married.'

Diana's eyes blazed. 'I knew it! I knew——'

'But that's all she knows, Diana!' His eyes watched her intently. 'I can promise you that.'

'I wouldn't believe one of your promises if it came gift-wrapped in million-pound notes!'

He gave a cynical laugh. 'You never were the mercenary type.'

'No,' she said angrily under her breath, 'but I was unquestionably a fool, and now I'm really paying for it, aren't I?'

Conor watched her, his face hard.

'How could you have told her, Conor?' Diana's voice was low and filled with emotion. 'How could you?'

'I had to tell her,' he said deeply. 'She'd already guessed.'

'When? When did you tell her?'

'Does it matter?' His brows rose. 'It's nothing to do with her. She can't interfere and she certainly wouldn't try.'

'But she *has* interfered!' Diana said angrily. 'She has! Look at what's happened since I signed to do this wretched picture!'

'Come on, Diana,' he said flatly, 'it's a good script, a good cast, good crew...' he laughed '...great director, and a very big budget. We can't go wrong—not unless you play prima donna from start to finish!'

'I might just do that!' Diana said angrily. 'I'm very tempted to make everybody concerned very sorry that they ever twisted my arm into doing this rotten——'

'I don't advise that, Diana,' Conor growled. 'I really don't.'

Her eyes raked him bitterly. 'Don't tell me—you'd soon knock me into shape if I tried it!'

He gave a sardonic smile. 'What do you think?' he asked softly, and there was a long tense silence while she stood very still and just hated him. Conor moved towards her again, took her chin in one hand and lifted her face. 'My darling. I have a job to do. I can't allow our personal feelings to get in the way of it.'

Her mouth trembled. 'Then why did you take this contract in the first place?'

'Because you were twenty-four,' he bit out thickly. 'Because the injunction was over. Because I wanted to have you close to me. Because I wanted to torment you, take revenge on you, make love to you, make you half

crazy with the kind of madness that only lovers know...'
his eyes darkened, his voice roughening '...I couldn't
turn it down, Diana. I couldn't. I had to work you out
of my system, even if it killed me, so I took this job and
now I'm going to take you. Piece by unwilling piece.
Step by passionate step. And I'll share your hatred, your
madness, your fear, your excitement, your passion...'

'Conor, it'll kill us both!' she said hoarsely, shaking
in his arms.

'I don't care!' he said under his breath. 'I have to do
it or go insane! You're in my blood, in my soul—you're
everything I've ever loved and everything I've ever hated,
and I'll have you, Diana, if I have to throw us both into
hell to get you!'

'That's what it'll come to!' she returned. 'Don't you
see we're already halfway to the abyss?'

'Yes!' he said harshly. 'And it's about time we took
another step into it!' His hands gripped her shoulders
tightly as he pulled her against him, and she was so surprised that she just gasped, clutching his biceps and
swaying, struggling to retain her balance.

But when his mouth came down passionately over hers
she started to moan, to struggle, and her fight infuriated
him.

'It's only a kiss!' he bit out thickly, eyes flashing.
'Must you fight me every time we touch?'

'Yes!' she hissed, struggling. 'I won't go into the
darkness with you, Conor! I won't!'

'Because you're afraid!' he said angrily. 'But you have
to conquer that fear.'

'Why do I have to?' Her eyes blazed with passionate
anger. 'Because it suits you to think it? You really are
a selfish bastard, Conor Slade, and I'd rather die than
ever give in to your unwanted demands again!'

Rage flared in his eyes. 'Unwanted demands?' he repeated tightly, then shouted, 'Unwanted demands?'

Diana jumped, eyes startled.

'You little bitch!' he bit out, then he was hurling her
on to the couch, fury in his face as he pinned her down

on it, the hoarse cries for mercy she gave ruthlessly ignored.

'Don't!' she screamed, but his hard mouth was already closing over hers and the sharp heat of excitement was pulsating in her veins as she moaned beneath his hard body and the onslaught of that demanding, passionate mouth.

'Unwanted demands?' he said hoarsely as he kissed her ruthlessly. 'Unwanted, are they? Well, let's just see how much you can take!' His hands went to the shoulders of her dress and tugged it down.

'Oh, God!' Diana bucked fiercely, gasping, eyes blazing. 'Don't you do that . . . don't you dare!'

Her breasts were bared and they were both panting for breath, staring down at her erect pink nipples and the sweat that clung to her flushed skin, trickling between her breasts.

'Yes!' Conor bit out thickly, and one hand grasped her bare breast. 'Let's see how much you can take!'

She cried out with fierce, furious pleasure as his hand fondled her breast, and suddenly his hard, hot mouth was covering hers, burning her as he kissed her with rough sounds of excitement, his strong hand hard on her breast, fondling the erect nipple and sending sharp needles of sexual excitement through her.

'Let's see how much you can take . . .' he whispered again, and his strong hand pushed up the skirts of her dress, slid up her cream-stockinged thighs and rested, as he struggled to breathe, on the creamy flesh of her thigh just above the stocking top.

Diana gasped for breath, panting beneath him, and when his kiss drove her back against the bed she went with it, emotions crackling all around her soul as the demons clamoured inside her and she moaned hoarsely, her slim thighs parting as he thrust one strong leg between them. It was all so natural, so right, so in keeping with the floodwaves of emotion. His mouth passionate on hers, her hands thrusting in his black hair, their thighs intertwining, his spine flexing as he bore down on her, her bare breasts covered in sweat as his hands slid over them and she heard the fierce sounds of rough, hectic pleasure he made as he touched her. When she felt his hand again on her bare thigh, she felt his fingers slide over the sweat-soft skin, and the need for total release suddenly began to drive into her, rolling into her soul like a hard iron spring in her belly that needed to snap and explode and send her spinning into dark, delicious chaos.

Chaos, she thought blindly, her mouth sliding against his: oh, yes, chaos...give me that chaos...that release...send me screaming into the abyss and let me hit the bottom of that black pit and all this will end.

'Unbutton my shirt!' Conor commanded, his voice shaking as he raised his head and she saw sweat on his eyelids. 'Unbutton it!'

She wanted to. She stared at his chest and she wanted to push that white shirt off, see the tanned hair-roughened flesh and run her fingers hungrily over it, press her breasts against it and hear him go wild with the need for release, see him shake as he shed his clothes, feel herself burn as he took her and...

The scent of danger was suddenly filling her nostrils and as she stared at Conor she realised how close she was to that abyss, how close to chaos and to hell.

'Unbutton it!' he said again, fiercely. 'Oh, God, Diana...I can't wait much longer! I've got to——'

'No.' Her voice was piercing enough to silence him.

For a long moment they just stared at each other. Diana was tense, lying beneath him without moving, her eyes blazing suddenly with pain and fear: not rage. The rage had all gone long ago. Dissipated into ruinous desire. All that was left was pain, and the fear of overstepping that line, that line that stood between her and chaos.

'Don't stop it now, Diana,' Conor warned in a tense voice, 'don't stop it——'

'I must,' she said, her voice strained as she met his gaze and did not blink. 'I must.'

He breathed harshly, closed his eyes, then flashed them open again and said shakingly, 'You were with me all the way! You wanted it as much as I did! You——'

'No!' she cried hoarsely, and then the tears stung her eyes and she squeezed them shut, her hands going to her face.

Conor was staring at her, struggling too for self-control. 'You mustn't turn back, Diana,' he said under his breath. 'You mustn't! We were almost there. I had you, I had you and you would have gone through with it!'

'Never!' she whispered, tears scalding her cheeks.

Conor's mouth twisted with pent-up desire and he bit out, 'You lying little bitch! You want me and you damned well know it!'

Diana closed her eyes and sobbed silently, unable to look him in the face.

There was a long silence while he watched her. Then his voice said harshly, 'Don't cry...Diana, don't...' His hand touched her cheek and came away wet.

'I can't help it!' Diana whispered through her tears. 'I'm so afraid Conor, and I can't bear it.'

'What are you afraid of?' he asked deeply, stroking her hair. 'The way you feel?'

Her eyes opened, lashes wet as she studied him in silence, her heart thudding.

Conor's eyes were very blue, very dark. 'It's too powerful, isn't it?' he said, his voice low. 'And it makes you feel you really are hurtling into hell.'

'Yes...' she said huskily. 'But more than that. I—I know it's wrong, because it's so impossible to control. And it only happens when...when you touch me. Like this...' She lowered her lashes and tentatively reached a hand out to stroke his hard chest in a shakily seductive way.

Conor inhaled sharply. 'Oh, yes,' he agreed thickly, 'that's when it makes you start to lose control...!'

Diana's eyes flashed and she withdrew her hand, saying hoarsely, 'It's only a physical attraction and I won't give in to it, do you hear me? I won't, I won't, I won't!'

He studied her in angry silence for a moment, then he said gruffly, 'You will, Diana! You will by the time

this damned film is finished, because I intend to make
you give in to it in the most passionate way!'

There was a silence while he studied her with hard,
determined eyes to make sure she had understood completely that there was no way out, and she had: her
breathing was erratic, her heartbeat pounding and her
limbs quivering with heat. She couldn't have spoken if
her life had depended on it.

Conor suddenly released her and got to his feet, raking
a hand through his thick black tousled hair as he
straightened, turning his back to her, his body as hard
and desirable as ever.

'I'll see you tomorrow at dawn for the first scene,' he
said, his eyes restless as he watched her haul the dress
back up over her bare breasts, flushing as she did so,
bitterly aware of his gaze. 'And if there are any more
prima donna tantrums I'll give you a repeat performance of this that will take the roof off the back of your
head. Understand?'

Her eyes were bitterly resentful. 'I understand!' she
flung, as though it were accusation enough in itself.

Conor smiled sardonically and left the trailer, blowing
her a mocking kiss as he went.

She hated herself for wanting him. Hated herself for
knowing it, deep down, and fought it bitterly, terrified
of what he would do if he ever realised how her traitor-
ous body secretly clamoured for him.

Diana turned on to her front, buried her face in her
hands and wept.

CHAPTER FIVE

FOR the next three days, Diana only saw Conor during
filming. She was up every morning at dawn, in make-
up by five and in front of the cameras by six, as the
early morning light began to shine gold over the bleached
French land.

Conor worked her like the tyrant he was. But, more
than that, he demanded her very best, and she gave it,

the chemistry between them flaring up into a sizzling combination that made every moment of her presence on celluloid electric.

On Saturday she had the day off along with the rest of the crew. Conor was filming the ballroom scene tonight, and he was supervising the crew as they 'redecorated' the ballroom to fit in with the film plot.

She spent the day lazily, talking to Geoff as they sat in the shade of the olive grove, drinking cold lemonade and agreeing with each other on what an absolute slave-driver Conor was.

'Have you been near the ballroom yet?' Geoff asked her. 'I passed it on my way out here, and all I could hear was Conor shouting orders.'

'All that time in the army,' Diana agreed, adjusting her sunglasses.

'Oh, that's right,' Geoff frowned, 'someone told me he was ex-SAS. Can't say I'm surprised. He's a pretty ruthless character, isn't he?'

'Yes,' Diana said huskily, shivering inside.

Geoff studied her. 'You seem to know him quite well. I don't suppose you've worked with him before, have you?'

'No,' she said, shaking her head, 'never! But I did know him before this film, yes.'

'Oh?' His pale brows drew in a frown. 'Very well?'

'We...' she cleared her throat, heart thudding '... we were very good friends...'

There was a little silence. 'Lovers?' Geoff asked deeply.

Diana caught her breath, staring at him, flushing as she said hotly, 'Geoff, for goodness' sake!'

'OK, OK!' He held up slim hands. 'No offence meant!'

'Geoff, I'm not offended,' Diana said quickly, 'but it really isn't the kind of question you should ask. Certainly as we're only colleagues and——' She broke off as a warm breeze stirred the olive trees and a piece of dust blew into her eye. 'Oh, damn!' Her hand flew to her eyes, felt it water, and winced, rubbing it furiously. 'Got something in my eye...'

'Let me see.' Geoff leant towards her, frowning, and Diana opened her watering eyes, staring blankly at the azure sky as Geoff fished out the offending speck. 'All gone,' he said gently, watching her, his face very close.

'Thanks,' Diana said, and looked at him.

Suddenly, he leant forwards and brushed a kiss on her mouth with his lips. 'Sorry,' he said huskily as Diana gasped in surprise. 'Had to do it...couldn't stop myself!'

Diana stared at him for a moment, then said quickly, 'That's OK, Geoff. But I—I must be getting in now. I have to be in make-up in half an hour...'

That was unfortunate, Diana realised as she went up the stairs to her room. Geoff was a very nice man, and she loved his company, but the last thing she wanted at the moment was for him to try and start some kind of on-location love-affair with her.

When she got to her room, she was astonished to find Eleanor there.

'Oh!' She stared at her guardian standing by the french doors. 'Hello. What are you doing here?'

Eleanor turned, tight-mouthed. 'I came to discuss my work tonight as an extra in the ballroom scene. Someone told me you were in your room. I stood on the balcony for a few minutes.'

'I see,' Diana said, closing the door and walking towards her.

'Your balcony has a splendid view,' Eleanor said coldly. 'I could see you and that young man quite clearly as you kissed.'

Diana stiffened, lifting her head. 'I had something in my eye. Geoff took it out and——'

'Kissed you,' Eleanor said flatly.

She moistened her lips. 'It wasn't something I encouraged.'

'Encouraged!' Eleanor said tightly, 'You don't even know you're doing it! You sit there and flaunt your body, flutter your eyelashes, pout at men, speak to them in that breathy voice and——'

'Oh, for God's sake!'

'It's true,' Eleanor said and looked out of the window. 'Still, I suppose that young man is a lot better than Conor Slade! If you have to behave like a tramp, I'd rather you chose Geoffrey Hastings than Conor Slade! Slade is trouble. Always has been, always will be. And he's only after one thing—don't you forget it.'

Diana counted to ten, moved to her dressing-table, picked up her hairbrush, ran it through her long, silken blonde hair, and, as the light flashed on it, Eleanor turned to look back at her.

'Your hair is so pretty like that,' said Eleanor.

Diana cleared her throat. 'Hadn't you better go down to wardrobe? They're fitting all the extras' costumes...'

Eleanor sighed. 'Must I really? I find it all so frightfully vulgar...'

Later, Diana went down to make-up. Her nerves were stretched to breaking-point. Everyone chattered gaily around her, but all she could think of was Conor and his need for revenge.

The ballroom was a dazzling blaze of scarlet and gold. The Sarcaronne unicorn crest was embroidered on a red canopy above three red-gold thrones on the raised stage. All the extras were there, talking at one end of the room, cameras, cables, vast arc lights, and crew.

Diana walked in slowly, red velvet dress hugging her slender figure, her shoulders left bare, a diamond and ruby choker around her white throat.

'I might have known you'd take my breath away,' Conor's dark, obsessive voice said. 'Can't you ever look anything less than superb?'

Diana flushed, aware that he himself looked magnificent in a black evening suit.

'Geoff seems to agree with me, too.' Conor's voice had a threatening tone as he blocked her path. 'I saw you on the lawn together. That was a tender little kiss he gave you. I was tempted to punch his handsome——'

'Geoff is my drama coach,' she said quickly. 'I got something in my eye this afternoon and he——'

'He just had to kiss your mouth to make it better,' Conor said tightly. 'Yes, it was all quite clear from where I stood!'

'Ready to roll, sir!' said the assistant director.

Conor turned, mouth hardening. 'Places, people!' He turned back to Diana, said under his breath, 'We'll continue this conversation at the first break in filming! You'd better have a good explanation for kissing another man, Diana, or I'll teach you a lesson you'll never forget!'

He strode away, and Diana struggled to keep calm as they began filming, though her heart was leaping with panic, and she knew her eyes kept flickering towards Conor as the lights blazed over her and the cameras rolled.

Trumpets blasted as the King and Queen walked in, and Diana followed them into shot. They mounted the red stage, sat on the red-gold thrones, and equerries carried the symbols of power contained in a long red box with three compartments.

Filming broke for the first time at ten o'clock.

'OK!' Conor called. 'Fifteen minutes, everyone!'

Diana felt the perspiration break out on her face, her eyes darting to him as he moved towards her. At once, she tried to make her way to the cofee trolleys wheeled in at the entrance.

'No coffee for you, Diana!' Conor blocked her path, smarter than her and smiling coldly with it. 'We have something to discuss—remember?'

He took her wrist in a biting grip and marched her across the ballroom towards the small red antechamber behind the throne area, whirling her inside and slamming the door behind him.

'Tell me about Geoff Hastings!' he said under his breath.

Diana faced him across that red room, her heart pounding. 'There's nothing to tell!'

Rage flared in his eyes. 'Tell me!'

She jumped, staring. 'Conor, for God's sake, we're only friends! He kissed me, but I didn't encourage him, and——'

'You didn't encourage him!' he bit out, eyes fierce. 'No man is safe with you!'

'Don't be ridiculous! You're practically the only man I've ever——' Her face ran with scarlet colour. 'I mean—the only boyfriend I've——'

'Right!' He shot forwards, eyes blazing, gripping her shoulders with hard hands. 'Me! And I'm damned if I'll stand aside and watch you give Geoff Hastings something you won't give me!'

'But I didn't!' she denied, shaking. 'I swear it!'

'He kissed you! I saw him kiss you!'

'Yes...!' She could feel herself being dragged into the maelstrom of his eyes. 'But I didn't kiss him, Conor! I just got kissed and that's a different matter!'

There was a brief tense silence. His heart was thudding as she rested her hands on his hard chest.

'Yes,' he said under his breath, 'it's a very different matter. But I didn't know you were quite so experienced, Diana!'

'I'm not...' she whispered, staring at his mouth. 'But I'm learning fast since you came back and——'

'Too fast!' he said thickly. 'And you're taking lessons from any man who'll give them to you!'

'No! The lessons I've learnt have been taught by you, Conor!'

His hands bit into her shoulders. 'Convince me!'

Her mind spun. 'I...I'd forgotten what a kiss could be until you came back...' God, was she really saying these things? Was her heart going to bang even faster than this? 'I—I remember what it is to be kissed...to be wanted...to—to want...'

'How can I believe that?' he said hoarsely. 'I saw you kiss the bastard! I say you do it!'

'He kissed me—I didn't kiss him!'

'Yes, and I'm always the one who kisses you, Diana!' he said roughly. 'You never kiss me back—you just submit and then run!' His hands dragged her against him, pressed her body close to his and he said under his breath, 'Well, this one time, Diana—this one time, you'll damned well kiss me back and *prove* that you know the difference between kissing and getting kissed!'

His dark head swooped, and as his hard mouth closed over hers, Diana felt that rush of excitement, let her mouth open beneath his, let herself moan out loud with pleasure, and heard his swift intake of breath as his kiss deepened to a burning, hungry triumph.

They clung together, and she revelled in the growing pleasure of thrusting her hands into his thick black hair, running her shaking fingers over his strong neck, pushing his passion to new heights as she tentatively, shakingly, slid her hands on to his chest and splayed them there, loving the feel of his hard-thudding heart.

'Oh, God, yes!' Conor muttered, desperation in his voice as he buried his mouth in hers, and as they clung together the dark obsessive passion flared up between them, engulfing them in the maelstrom they had always shared.

When the door opened, neither of them heard it.

Diana was moaning under the onslaught of his mouth, her head back and her mouth passionate beneath his.

'You little whore!' Eleanor's voice blazed from the doorway.

There was a split second of appalled realisation as Diana's eyes snapped open and she stared at her guardian standing in scarlet at the doorway, her blue eyes blazing with contempt.

'Eleanor!' Diana whispered, swaying, face white.

Conor had dragged his mouth from hers, face darkly flushed as he turned with a quick intake of breath to stare at Eleanor, too.

'I knew it!' Eleanor was saying fiercely, walking towards them. 'I knew the minute my back was turned that little trollop would be back in your arms and back in your bed!'

'Oh, God...' Diana was whispering, shivering with shock as she stumbled back from Conor. 'Oh, my God!'

'Now just a minute, Eleanor!' Conor bit out, eyes
flashing. 'You had no business coming in here and certainly no business——'

'One man isn't enough for you!' Eleanor blazed,
shaking with rage. 'Oh, no, you have to have as many
as you can get, just like your mother, you little tramp,
you little——'

'Don't speak about my wife like that!' Conor shouted,
furious.

'What on earth is going on?' Georgina had suddenly
appeared in the doorway, and took in the scene at once,
freezing where she stood in her magnificent scarlet dress.
'Oh, my God!' she said on a whisper, then stepped into
the room and closed the door behind her.

'Get out, Georgina!' Eleanor whirled on her angrily.
'This is nothing to do with you and I——'

'It's my film company, my director and my star!'
Georgina said icily, green eyes blazing contempt at
Eleanor. 'I believe that gives me the power in this
château, Eleanor, and power, as we both know, is all!'

'You have no power here, Georgina!' Eleanor bit out.
'Not over Diana! Not over that wanton little trollop...'
Her blue eyes stabbed at Diana across the room. 'Look
at her! Look at her, all of you! My God, if I hadn't seen
it with my own eyes I would never have believed it!'

'We were married!' Conor bit out tightly. 'We've
already made love long, long ago, Eleanor, and this is
mild, believe me, to what you would have seen had you
walked in on our wedding night!'

'Don't disgust me!' Eleanor said fiercely. 'You only
married her for this! And it's all you'll get, let me tell
you! It's all she's good for! Didn't you see her, any of
you, seducing that blond drama coach in the gardens
this afternoon? And now this! Now this disgusting
display of——'

'Diana is an adult woman!' Georgina interrupted, face
icy and implacable. 'It's time you accepted that and
stopped trying to kill her with your lunatic rantings on
the subject of sex. She and Conor were in love. They
got married and——'

'You knew!' Eleanor blazed, beside herself with rage. 'This has been a set-up from the beginning! You knew about Conor and that's why you hired him!'

'Georgina and I are old friends,' Conor said angrily. 'She agreed to help me get close enough to Diana to find out what really happened!'

'And did Diana know?' Eleanor shouted, turning to stare at Diana with dislike flaring from her eyes. 'I'll bet she did! I'll bet she's been in on this from the word go!' She started to move towards Diana, saying under her breath, 'Such a liar...such a wanton, immoral, un-principled little liar!'

'No...!' Diana denied on a whisper, shaking from head to foot. 'No!'

'You're just like my sister!' Eleanor shouted, and slapped Diana across the face, blue eyes blazing with hatred.

Diana slid slowly and silently to the floor, and the red room, the red dresses, and Conor Slade running towards her with a shout of concern were the last things she saw...

When she awoke she was lying on her bed, and she slowly let her eyelids open, gazing up at the white lace canopy of the four-poster, and noticing for the first time that there were tiny flowers embroidered into the white lace. Then she became aware of another presence and turned her head quickly, gasping as she saw Conor Slade sitting on the bed watching her with a grim expression.

Suddenly she remembered, and as she did she gasped in horror, sitting upright, saying 'Oh, my God! Eleanor! She——'

'Lie down,' he said flatly, and forced her down again, his strong hands relentless as they pushed her back on to the bed. 'You've had a shock and you must rest.'

Diana stared up at him through her lashes. 'Where's Eleanor?'

'Georgina's looking after her.'

She nodded. 'And the film?'

'Postponed until tomorrow at eleven.'

She moistened her lips. 'I...I fainted. Didn't I?' Her
eyes slid to his face again and she said huskily, 'You
must think me very foolish...I just couldn't help it.'

'Most women in your position would have fainted,'
he said coolly, 'don't you think?'

Her mouth trembled at his kindness and she covered
her face with shaking hands, saying hoarsely, 'Oh,
God...I couldn't bear it! It was just like that last time...'

'After we were married?'

Diana tensed, looking up at him with pain-filled eyes.
'Yes...'

He nodded, mouth hard. 'Tell me about it. Tell me
exactly what happened.'

She moistened her lips and stammered, 'I...I promised
I'd never tell anyone!'

'But now you know you must tell me? That you've
hidden it for too long?' Conor enquired coolly.

She hesitated, then closed her eyes and nodded. 'I
don't think I can stand living like this any more.'

He studied her for a moment, then took a glass of
brandy from the bedside table and handed it to her.
'Here. Brandy. It'll steady you.'

Obediently she took the glass and drank. 'It was the
morning after the wedding,' she said, astonished to find
the words tripping off her tongue without any real im-
pediment. 'You'd driven into the village to get some milk.
Do you remember?'

'Yes,' he said deeply, watching her, 'we couldn't have
any coffee and the nearest farm was further than the
village.'

'Eleanor must have been watching the cottage,' Diana
said huskily, 'because it was only five minutes after you'd
left that she knocked on the door. I thought it was you,
so I answered it at once.'

He nodded, watching her as she hesitated. 'Go on.'

'Eleanor was livid. She just looked me up and down
with contempt and I saw myself through her eyes and
felt such guilt...such shame...'

Conor's face hardened. 'She'd flown over from New
York? How the hell did she manage it so fast?'

'Concorde,' Diana murmured. 'Sophie's parents had telephoned her in New York as soon as they'd read my elopement note. Eleanor got the first flight back, arrived in London...' her brows lifted '...probably at around the time you and I were actually married...'

'Fast work,' he commented, mouth tightening.

'Of course,' Diana said thickly, 'I knew it would be a shock to her. The elopement, I mean. But she'd always said when I got married it would be because I fell in love, so I...' She broke off, face burning, unable to look at him, then stammered haltingly, 'So, when I did, I naturally assumed it would all be all right. That—that Eleanor would eventually see how romantic it was to elope! And to elope to the place I was born...Ireland.'

'But Eleanor didn't find it remotely romantic?' Conor said flatly, mouth hard.

'No. She pushed past me into the cottage, and looked around at it.' She shuddered, drank some more brandy and said hoarsely, 'She kept looking at things...you know that way she does...with that expression of absolute contempt. And I—I felt so ashamed of everything. Ashamed of the cottage and of my marriage to you and——'

'And then?'

Diana swallowed hard. 'And then she turned on me with such an icy look on her face that I...I just felt so terrified. Like a child who's done something terribly, terribly wrong. She—she said I looked like a whore and had behaved like a whore and that that was why you had married me: for nothing but sex.'

Conor's eyes blazed, but he said tightly, 'Go on.'

'Well...' Diana gave a hoarse laugh, tears burning her eyes. 'I knew what was coming next! And sure enough she said it: "I won't have another Allannah Sullivan in my family!" she said, and I just felt so cold inside, so cold and alone...'

'Right,' Conor said deeply, watching her with intense blue eyes. 'Who is Allannah Sullivan?'

'My mother,' she answered in surprise, and stared at him.

Conor stared back, blue eyes glittering with shocked realisation. 'You mean—you weren't adopted by a stranger?'

'No,' she said simply, 'Eleanor is my mother's sister.'

Conor studied her for a long moment. Then he said deeply, 'Tell me about Allannah Sullivan.'

Diana's lashes flickered. 'I don't really know much about her, Conor.'

'Were you a baby when she died?'

'I was a year old.'

'What about your father?'

'He died with her,' she said with a sigh. 'They were on a flight from Dublin to London and it crashed into the Irish Sea. Eleanor was the only relative prepared to take me on, and so I became her legal ward when I was thirteen months old.'

Conor frowned. 'Does Eleanor ever talk of her?'

'Only with hatred,' Diana said huskily, shrugging.

'Do you have any idea why?' Conor asked with a frown.

'She never speaks of it. I know something must have happened, but ...'

Conor nodded. 'OK. We can find that out another time. For the moment ... it's enough for me to know what's been at the bottom of this all along.'

Diana looked up at him and her mouth trembled. 'I can't help looking like her, can I?'

'No,' he said deeply, holding her gaze, his eyes serious, 'and I'm very glad you do, because I think you're beautiful.'

'But they hated her so!' Diana whispered. 'And when Eleanor was at the cottage that day, she said it. Just what she said in that red room a moment ago!'

Conor's mouth parted. 'That's why you fainted!'

'It reminded me so much of that other time; the last time I was with you and she caught me.'

'But we were married, Diana,' he said tightly. 'You should have told her that we——'

'I did!' she protested. 'I really did, Conor! I held up my wedding-ring and said, "But it's all right, Mama!

We're married! We're man and wife now and Conor loves me!"'

'And what did she say to that?'

'She said I'd only married you because it gave me the opportunity to get away from her and start having lovers.'

'What?'

Diana nodded. 'That's what she said. And when I said, "No, you're wrong! I love Conor..."' She broke off, flushing and lowering her lashes, finishing huskily, 'When I said all that sort of thing, she just stared at me for a moment, looked me up and down with such contempt and dislike and then shouted, "You're just like my sister!" and slapped me across the face.'

Conor's eyes closed for a second, and he said deeply, 'What happened then?'

Diana frowned and said shakily, 'I...I don't really know. It was like being in a dream then. I just looked at the cottage and it suddenly seemed the most awful, sordid place in the world. Eleanor said I was to go upstairs and pack my things immediately because we would both be flying back to London that afternoon.'

'And so you packed?' he said under his breath.

'Yes...' She nodded her blonde head '...I didn't even argue with her. I was just desperate suddenly to get out of the cottage and put everything right again. I remember being in the bedroom, though. I...I remember staring at the rumpled bed and feeling sick...feeling so sordid and cheap and appalled by what I'd done. I remember thinking how vile reality was; and how stupid I'd been to think eloping with you was romantic when it had turned into ashes in my hands. I remember looking out of the window and seeing Connemara, seeing Ireland, and knowing that I didn't love Ireland any more: I hated it! I hated it so much that I couldn't bear to ever see it again, and I hated you even more than I hated Ireland!' She stopped with a gasp of breath, closing her eyes, and whispered, 'I just had to get out, Conor! I had to leave you and I had to leave the cottage and I had to leave Ireland! I would have been physically sick if I'd stayed in that cottage a moment longer!' Her mouth compressed, eyes opening as she said fiercely, 'So I dressed and packed in three minutes flat, and ran down the stairs to join Eleanor in the living-room.'

'And the note?' Conor asked flatly.

'Eleanor had a piece of paper and pen waiting. She told me what to write. I wrote it. She told me to sign it. I signed it. She told me to go out and get in the car. I went out and got in the car.' She drew in her breath, trembling. 'I didn't even look back as we drove away! I just shut my eyes and prayed we wouldn't pass you on the road!'

Conor got to his feet, thrusting his hands into the pockets of his black trousers and turned away. The black evening jacket was hung over the back of a chair. His strong-muscled back strained the white shirt he wore at the shoulders.

'You went straight to the Sullivan Manor in Hampshire?' he asked.

'Yes.' Diana nodded. 'Eleanor said she wasn't going to let me out of her sight ever again. I obviously couldn't be trusted, I'd been a liar since the moment I was born, and I was just like——'

'Your mother,' he said deeply.

Diana gave a husky laugh, commenting, 'I was going to say Allannah Sullivan!'

'I know,' he replied quietly, mouth hard, and looked at her through black lashes, 'but you must stop thinking of her as that. Think only of her as your mother. Always. Even if you have to correct yourself constantly. She was your *mother*, Diana, and you must see her as that.'

'I...I know...' Diana said huskily, lowering her lashes. 'It's just so difficult after such a long time...'

'Yes,' he said.

Diana looked down, fingers plucking at the lace coverlet, and thought of her mother, of Allannah, and wondered if she had really been as bad as Eleanor and Claudius had always said she was. It felt so odd to think of her as mother: so very odd.

'It's difficult,' she said again, and looked up through her lashes to add, 'It seems almost terrifying! To say that word and say it about her...'

'That's just the effect of Eleanor's behaviour towards you since you were born,' said Conor deeply. 'It will fade the more you think of Allannah and say "mother".'

Diana laughed huskily. 'It...it seems toweringly big, that word, all of a sudden! "Mother"!' Her blue eyes danced and she drew a shaky breath. 'I feel very brave, just saying it!'

Conor smiled.

Diana met his gaze and felt breathless, looking away at once, her heart thudding.

'So when did Eleanor arrange the world cruise on the QE2?' Conor asked coolly.

'As soon as we got back,' Diana replied. 'It was very short notice, of course, but luckily they did have some cabins spare. Eleanor booked in and got a flight from London to Marseilles so we could join the cruise within the week.'

'And she never told you I tried to see you.'

'No.'

Conor nodded, mouth hard, and was silent for a long moment. Then he looked up at her and said, 'When did you decide to dye your hair blonde?'

Diana's lashes flickered. 'It...it was Eleanor's idea.'

'Ah...' He studied her, blue eyes piercing. 'What did she do? Hold your head over a sink and pour a bottle of household bleach over it?'

'Yes...' Diana said huskily.

'What?' Conor bit out, eyes leaping.

'We had a row!' Diana protested. 'I...I said some——'

'My God, I can't believe anyone would do such a thing!' Conor came towards her, sank on to the bed. 'Diana, if only I'd known!'

Diana's mouth trembled as she stared at him and murmured, 'I...I guess it was a pretty awful thing to do to me, wasn't it?'

'Darling!' he said deeply, and took her in his arms, stroking her hair, breathing in the scent of it. 'Your beautiful hair...'

Diana sobbed silently on his strong neck. 'I...I was so terrified of her! And so terrified of looking like...like...' she closed her eyes '...my mother.'

'I take it your mother was slim, petite, curvaceous and sexy?' Conor said deeply, still holding her.

'Yes...' Diana nodded, tears squeezing through her lids.

'While Eleanor is tall, thin and slightly masculine,' Conor said coolly.

'Masculine?' Diana pulled back and stared at him. 'Eleanor?'

'Yes,' he said lightly, 'haven't you ever noticed? She's very businesslike, isn't she? Cold, precise, formal and rather hard. Very opinionated, too, and fond of giving orders.'

'I...I suppose she is a bit,' she admitted carefully, 'but don't you think she's terribly elegant, too? And clever?'

Conor raised dark brows and said deeply, 'Hating someone for looking like their natural mother isn't terribly clever, is it?'

She was silent for a moment as her mind dared to agree very, very hesitantly.

'Surely,' Conor went on, 'it would be more intelligent of her to simply accept it?'

Diana looked up at him through her dark lashes.

'After all,' he pointed out, 'you are your mother's daughter. You are slim, petite, curvaceous and...' he flashed wicked eyes at her '...ve-ry sexy!'

She blushed, laughing softly and lowering her lashes.

'So what's the point,' he asked quietly, 'of trying to turn a lioness into a tabby cat?'

Diana looked up hesitantly.

'All she's done is paint tabby stripes on you, put a collar around your neck and make you sit by the fire drinking milk.'

She laughed. 'Very flattering, Conor, but I...' She watched him carefully, hesitating, her voice husky as she said quickly, 'I think I see your point...'

'You do see my point,' he said deeply, watching her. 'Come on. Say it out loud.'

Diana blushed, a shoulder curving as she felt shyness overwhelm her. 'All right...I...I do see your point!'

Conor laughed, tilted her chin up to look at him. 'Hmm. Well, it's a start. One day, you'll be able to say it all out loud without feeling afraid, and by that time you'll have long black silky hair again, just as you did when I first met you.'

She buried her face in his shoulder and clung to him, feeling so much emotion that she could no longer work out whether she felt it for him or for the catastrophes of the past or whether she was just exhausted.

'And now?' Conor asked deeply, stroking her hair. 'How do you feel about me now? Now that this is all out in the open.'

She tensed, saying at once, 'I don't know! I'm confused! I don't know what I feel!'

'How can you not know what you really feel?' he demanded. 'You push me away with one hand and beckon with the other! Now, think about it and be direct with me. When I kiss you...' his gaze burnt her mouth as he stared at it and his voice deepened. '...when I touch you...here...' one hand cupped her breast '...how do you feel?'

She stared, dry-mouthed and whispered, 'I'm not going to tell you!'

'That's what you think!' he said under his breath, and his hand moved below her breast and he said softly, 'I can feel your heart racing. Why should that be?'

'Don't...' she whispered, heart banging as she stared into his eyes.

'But I'm going to,' he said softly, 'and we both know it.'

'But we don't both necessarily want it...'

'Then why are both our hearts stepping up the pace?'

She seemed locked into his blazing eyes. 'Maybe we're both tired...'

'Or excited.'

'Or rushing into disaster!'

'Now there's a possibility!' he said under his breath, and then his fingers moved slowly back to her breast.

'Don't...' she whispered, staring at his hard, sensual mouth.

'Why not, Diana?' He stroked her nipple into erect obedience beneath the bodice, seeing her face flush with arousal and hearing her gasp. 'How does that make you feel?'

'I don't know!' she said, voice throbbing with passion. 'But I don't like it!'

He removed his hand slowly from her breast and looked at her through those black lashes. 'Better?' he taunted softly.

'Oh, God!' she whispered helplessly, staring at that strong, dark-haired hand with a sense of deprivation.

'Ah...!' His eyes gleamed with dark threat, and he bent his head, hard mouth brushing softly against hers. 'Maybe I should just kiss you? Like this...' His mouth opened hers, probing it with slow, sensual skill.

Diana moaned softly, whispering, 'Oh, Conor...'

His mouth opened hers again, and the tortuous slowness was exquisite. 'You're kissing me back, my love...' he said softly against her mouth as he closed it again, brushing light kisses on her lips. 'Maybe I should go before it gets out of hand.'

She couldn't speak, her body on fire as she stared at him.

A slow smile touched his hard mouth. 'Or shall I carry on?'

'Yes...' she said, dry-mouthed, shocked by her own voice.

He moved slowly, and his hard mouth opened hers, still with that slow, sensual exploration, and, as his mouth ruined her until she was moaning, her hair spread across the pillow, she felt his hand move slowly, inexorably back to her breast, touching her through the red

velvet bodice, his strong fingers ruthlessly skilled and
unhurried.

'Conor...!' she was whispering against his mouth,
heart hammering. 'Conor!'

Slowly, he tugged the bodice down to bare one breast,
and Diana moaned, shivering, waiting, feeling the air
on her bare skin and rosy-tipped nipple. It took so long
to feel his strong fingers but when they finally slid over
her breast she gave a long, low moan of pleasure and
ached with building excitement as his fingers slowly
stroked her nipple.

'Oh...' she was moaning softly as he forced her to
wait. 'Oh, God...' and his hands were ruthlessly slow,
ruthlessly skilled, his mouth torturing her as she lay
spread across the bed in molten surrender to her master.

'You want me to stop?' he asked under his breath,
strong fingers stroking her nipples. 'Hmm?'

'No...' she whispered, body aching with tension and
excitement. 'No, don't stop...'

Slowly, he slid one strong thigh between her legs and
the slight pressure made her blood throb as she helplessly spread her legs beneath him and moaned against
that hard, skilled mouth.

'Oh, God!' Diana whispered as she felt the evidence
of his arousal pressing against her pulsating centre. 'Oh,
Conor...Conor!'

Suddenly he gave a rough sound of desperation, as
though he could stand it no more, and his mouth possessed hers with a demanding passion that swept her
breath away, made her cry out with fierce pleasure as
his hands grew harder on her breasts, and he suddenly,
swiftly lowered his dark head, breathing harshly, to close
his hot mouth around her nipple.

'Oh, God, I've wanted you for so long!' he said
thickly, and his strong hands were shaking as they pushed
up the long red velvet skirt of her gown to her slim black-
stockinged thighs. 'Oh, Diana...oh, yes, let me do this!'
and his strong fingers curved around her creamy upper
thighs where the black stockings ended and the sounds
he made were of a man near explosion, his teeth almost

clenching with desire as he raised his head to stare down at her splayed thighs and whispered, 'God help me, I've got to have you!' He drew a shaking breath and then his hands were unbuttoning his white shirt as he stared at her with eyes like black molten coals; whirlpools of emotion, of savage love and of chaos.

Diana stared at the tanned, hair-roughened chest, and her mouth went dry with longing and desire as she moaned and reached out to touch, her hands shaking on his skin as she heard his rough gasp of urgency as he pulled the shirt off and flung it to the floor.

Then he was breathing even more harshly as he unzipped the scarlet velvet gown and threw it aside, moaning as he stared down at her body, at her silken nudity and the black silk briefs and silk stockings.

Diana said hoarsely, 'Conor, don't!' and stared at him, her blue eyes fierce in her flushed face, torn suddenly between the ferocity of her arousal and the terror of chaos.

'Accept it!' he said thickly, and his hands shook on her thighs as he stared down at them, then back at her face. 'I'm going to make love to you because we both want it. More than that—we both damned well need it!'

Diana caught her breath as his mouth came back to hers, but it was no good: she was tensing with every passing second, and, as his harsh sounds of pleasure grew more frantic, as his hands pushed the black stockings from her legs and flung them alongside her dress, so the tension grew more, and with it grew the fear.

'Don't lose it, darling!' Conor said hoarsely, his mouth at her throat, sensing her withdrawal. 'No, no, not now! Don't let it take hold of you!'

'I—I'm trying!' she whispered, but, as his hands moved to her black silk briefs and his harsh sounds of urgency grew, so she felt the fear punch hard in her stomach just as Conor's strong tanned hand moved with shaking need to her buttocks.

'Oh, God!' he was saying thickly, harshly, gripping her. 'Oh, yes, I've got to...' and his hands went to the waistband of his black trousers, swiftly unzipping them, his heart thundering with desire.

'No!' Diana cried, jack-knifing up against his chest in panic and struggling to get away from him. 'No! No, Conor, I can't let you do it, I can't!'

'Don't refuse me now!' he said hoarsely, his arm gripping her semi-nude body against his. 'Please... my darling... the barrier is so invisible once you've taken it!'

'No!' she screamed, and began to fight in earnest, aware that she was inches from danger, her hands flailing in desperation to fight him off.

They struggled in bitter silence for a long time, Conor trying to catch her wrists, biting out angry words under his breath as she scratched and kicked her way to freedom, not even caring that she was almost naked, and pinned beneath him even though they both sat up, because he was sitting back on his heels right between her slender legs.

'All right, all right!' Conor bit out suddenly under his breath and his hands finally fastened around her wrists as he breathed deeply, saying, 'You've just had a terrible shock...you're not strong enough yet... I shouldn't have pushed you.'

Diana gave a long deep sigh of hoarse relief and opened her eyes, saying huskily, 'Conor, I'm so sorry. I must have seemed so eager for——' She broke off, biting her lip as a hot flush stung her cheeks. 'I—I mean it must have looked as though I——'

'Wanted to make love with me?' Conor drawled wryly. 'Hmm. Well, I'm afraid it did rather seem that way, darling!'

She flushed hotly and said, 'I felt so free...so un-afraid until you started to completely undress me.'

'Well, that's a start,' he said coolly, brows rising. 'That's something we can work on.'

'Oh...' she stared '...you mean you're going to stay around until——?'

'Why?' he interrupted, eyes narrowing. 'Don't you want me to?'

Diana moistened her lips, heart skipping. 'I—I'd like to know exactly what you're going to stay around for.'

He laughed softly. 'For more of this...' His hand stroked her bare shoulder, ran silkily down the curve of her naked spine. 'My God, Diana, if you only knew how our wedding night has tormented me over the years! You were so abandoned. The young woman with the brave, clean-scrubbed face and the boarding-school upbringing suddenly turned into a passionate woman.' He studied her, his eyes dark. 'And what a woman. You took even me by surprise. I knew you were a time-bomb waiting to be detonated, but when I did make that detonation, my God, you took my breath away. I'd expected you to be shy and hesitant, and you were at first, but after the first time...'

Diana stared at him in horror and the words flashed into her mind with lightning clarity: Eleanor was right! He does only want sex!

CHAPTER SIX

DIANA couldn't sleep that night. The events of the day and evening whirled in her mind like the Furies, and she tossed and turned in her bed, alternately hating Conor and loving him.

He had been sensitive and understanding; but he had also been cruel. And when he had told her how much he remembered their wedding night, how much he wanted to repeat the experience, and how exciting her passion had been, she had only been able to think that one, awful thought: Eleanor had been right.

Diana sighed, pushed back the bedclothes, got up and padded across the night-darkened room to the french windows. Stepping out on to the balcony, she breathed in the warm scented night air and listened to the crickets in the dark bushes below.

His lovemaking was as exciting as ever, and Diana hated herself for her overwhelming response, but was helpless. I want him, she thought in a moment of appalled understanding. I want him as much as he wants me, yet I know he doesn't love me.

Perhaps I *am* like Allannah, she thought, brows lifting. Like my mother... How many lovers had she had, after all? Would Diana ever find out? Eleanor had never actually told her anything about Allannah's life or the scandal that had obviously made Eleanor hate her so.

But it was something to do with men, Diana realised, tears stinging her eyes. Something to do with love and lovers.

She stood on the balcony in silence for a long time, thinking of her mother, of Allannah Sullivan and her dark, mesmeric beauty, of the black hair and passionate blue eyes that she had inherited, and the hot-blooded taste for men like Conor Slade that could ruin her forever.

Oh, God, she thought in agony: how can I live with this torment? To want a man who doesn't love me, and to know where that wanton road leads—only to self-destruction.

Tears burnt her eyes. And Conor wouldn't care. Conor wouldn't care if he saw her in such torture, agonising over her passionate need for him: that would be enough for Conor Slade. He would only want that; that and nothing else.

He certainly wouldn't want my stupid sentimental heart, she thought, a tear sliding down her pale, moonlit cheek. Didn't he say it himself tonight? His need for her, his need for revenge and his burning passion: all stemmed from that hot-blooded night when they had been married and had made love under the blood-red sky of Connemara.

Well, she thought angrily, he won't ever have that again. If she had to lie until her teeth dropped out, he would never, ever know just how much she wanted him to make love to her.

Next day, she woke up feeling half dead. She took a shower, then dressed in pale blue jeans and a white strappy sun-top. She hid the dark circles under her eyes with a pair of sunglasses.

At breakfast, everyone stared at her and whispered. Diana felt a fool. They had all witnessed that awful scene last night, and she was keen to get away from their knowing eyes.

After breakfast, she slipped into the grounds alone. As she crossed the cobbled courtyard, a horse clip-clopped in from the gate. Georgina sat astride it, aristocratic in black jacket and jodhpurs and white blouse, her hair held in a black net below her hard hat.

'Ah!' Georgina's brows rose as she saw Diana. 'If it isn't our Puccini heroine! How are you, my dear, after your performance in last night's grand opera?'

Diana flushed. 'I'm shattered, to be honest.'

'I'm not surprised.' The horse swished its tail. 'There were quite a few megawatts of emotion flashing around in that room. I didn't know Eleanor had it in her! Heavens, she's really rather passionate, isn't she?'

Diana stared at her, frowning, astonished at her words.

'I wonder why she hated your mother so much,' Georgina drawled, watching her closely. 'Have you ever asked her?'

'I . . .' Her mouth dried and she shook her head. 'No.'

'Perhaps it's time you did. But not just at the moment, darling.' She flashed wicked green eyes as she told her, 'I've just ridden back across the outer fields, and witnessed a quite touching little rendezvous between Eleanor and James Carthax!'

'James Carthax?' Diana's mouth dropped open. 'You don't mean the chief accountant?'

'I'm afraid so, darling!' Georgina laughed. 'They were only talking, of course, but I can scent a love-affair at fifty paces, and I'm utterly convinced that passion will flare between them!'

Diana laughed breathlessly, shaking her head. 'What makes you think they're on the brink of a . . . a love-affair?'

'They're both as lonely as each other,' said Georgina, 'and as bitter.' She alighted from her horse. 'Yes, life has been unkind to both of them. Poor James had a frightful experience with a rather unfaithful wife, you know.'

'Really?' Diana walked with her as Georgina led her horse into the stable, took off its saddle and started brushing it down. 'You know James quite well, then?'

'Oh, I know everyone on the team well,' she said with a brisk nod. 'Won't hire people unless they'll fit in on the team. A film is difficult enough if everyone gets on, but when they don't . . .!'

Diana studied her through her lashes. 'In that case, why did you throw Conor Slade and me together?'

There was a little silence. The horse snorted and Georgina's hand faltered as she brushed its coat, long lashes flickering for a moment.

'Darling,' she said gently, turning to her, 'I know you're going through hell with Conor. But it is rather a passionate sort of hell, isn't it?'

Her face flamed and she said huskily, 'I hate him!'

'Gosh, how frightfully encouraging!' Georgina laughed. 'And I don't blame you, darling. I hate him, too: he's so damned sexy!'

Diana caught her breath, staring.

Georgina smiled, eyes flashing past her. 'Don't you agree, Diana? How sexy Conor is?'

'Well,' she said, flushing furiously, 'I—I suppose he is very sexy, but I still hate him! He's an unprincipled, immoral——'

'Don't go on,' drawled a dark, angry voice behind her. 'My ego couldn't take it!'

Diana whirled, gasping to see Conor's powerful body blocking the light at the entrance to the stable, and her face burned as she looked at Georgina angrily and realised she had been tricked.

'Gosh, is that the time?' said Georgina, laughing. 'I simply must be off. Farewell, *mes amis*!' She slipped out of the stable, leaving the horse stamping one foot restlessly.

There was a long silence. Conor and Diana studied each other motionlessly, and she could scarcely breathe,

angry with herself for having betrayed her real feelings
so early.

'So,' Conor said under his breath, eyes hard, 'you hate
me again, do you?'

She tightened her lips and said quickly, 'I didn't make
any promises last night, Conor.'

'Didn't you?' He moved towards her, magnificently
sexy in blue jeans, a white shirt and a black silk unbuttoned waistcoat. 'I got a very different impression. Particularly when you kissed me goodnight!'

Her face flamed and she said hotly, 'I didn't have a
choice, did I? I had to kiss you! You were in my room,
on my bed and I was——'

'Helpless?' His eyes flashed a warning. 'You could
have asked me to leave at any time and——'

'Oh, don't make me laugh!' she said furiously,
backing. 'You know perfectly well that you never take
any notice of what I say! Especially when I'm alone with
you!'

Conor stopped, watching her with a grim expression.
'That isn't true, Diana. You had a bad experience last
night and I helped you through it.'

'You created it!' she accused bitterly.

His mouth hardened. 'Forgive me,' he said tightly,
'but I believe Eleanor created it.'

She looked away, her eyes bitter, and didn't know what
to say. How could she explain to him, her nemesis, just
what anger and pain was in her heart? To feel like this
for a man, to be so caught up in him, so involved, so
drawn, so passionate...and yet to know that he only
wanted sex! It was intolerable.

'Diana,' Conor said under his breath, touching her
face with one long hand, 'we spent a long time talking
last night. Talking—and making love. I thought we'd
come to an understanding. I thought we'd reached a new
stage of our relationship and——'

'Relationship!' she said bitterly, shaking her head. 'We
don't have a relationship, Conor. All we have is a
constant battle!'

His mouth tightened. 'Only because you won't stop fighting me.'

'Why should I?' she asked hoarsely. 'When you won't stop pushing me into the very acts of passion that made me leave you in the first place!' With a choked sob, she pushed past him and ran out into the sunlight, her feet clattering on the cobbled stone.

'Just a minute!' Conor's hand caught her wrist halfway across the courtyard and he whirled her to face him, blue eyes fierce. 'You can't do this, Diana! Not now! Not when we've finally reached a new point of understanding each other!'

'The only thing I understand,' she said shakily, tears stinging her eyes as she winced against the hot sunlight, 'is that you want to make love to me. That's all, Conor. Nothing more, nothing less.'

'Why shouldn't I want that?' he asked thickly. 'I feel such a need to touch you whenever I see you. To hold you as close as you can possibly get—and lovemaking is the absolute closest.'

She shook her blonde head. 'I don't want that…can't you understand how I feel?'

'But you *do* want it!' he said under his breath. 'You know you do. You said as much last night. My God, I almost couldn't find the self-control I needed so badly. I was on the edge, Diana. I should have made love to you but I didn't!'

'You're so thoughtful!' she said hoarsely, hating him.

'And do you know why I didn't?' His hands gripped her shoulders. 'Because of what we'd been through! Because you'd been honest, because you'd told me the truth at last…and because you'd lain in my arms and cried like a baby. How could I have forced myself on you in those circumstances?'

'Oh, I don't know, Conor,' she said huskily. 'It's never stopped you forcing yourself on me before!'

There was an electric silence. His eyes were furious. Diana looked into his face, her eyes pain-filled, and knew she had gone too far, but the pain and anger inside her were fighting for expression, and she knew Conor had

only ever wanted sex; what he had said last night had
proved it. His memories of their wedding were confined
to the bedroom. He didn't care if she had loved him, if
she had had silly romantic dreams at that time of how
happy they would be together, how much they had to
share, how dark-haired and passionate their children
would be... all he cared about was his time in bed with
her, and she hated him bitterly for the destruction of
her dreams and illusions about love.

'How can you say that?' Conor asked, staring at her.
'How can you say it and look me in the face?'

'Easily, Conor,' she said with a hoarse sob as she
pulled away from him, 'because it's true!'

She turned and ran back into the château, tears
stinging her eyes as she raced along the marble corridors
towards the make-up room. No matter how much it hurt
she would have to keep rejecting him, have to keep deny-
ing her feelings. She had been so badly hurt already—
more pain from Conor would only lead to her
destruction.

Filming the end of the ballroom scene was a nightmare.
Conor took every opportunity to pull her up short when
her acting wasn't up to scratch. She knew that on each
occasion he was right. Her emotions were so fraught that
she could barely remember her lines. But it made the
hurt even worse, and she was very glad when it was over.

Eleanor did not appear for work as an extra, and,
although Diana was worried by her absence, she was also
relieved. The thought of another argument with her was
out of the question. She was too emotionally exhausted
as it was, and her main focus of concern was Conor: as
it had always been.

After filming, she changed back into her jeans and
went out into the gardens again to escape Conor. He was
supervising the removal of the scenery from the
ballroom, and as she walked past the eight open sets of
french doors all she could hear was his dark voice issu-
ing orders.

'He's even worse today, isn't he?' Geoff suddenly appeared beside her and she turned, surprised. 'Sorry,' he

said with a wry smile, 'I saw you come out and I followed you.'

Diana looked at the ballroom doors and felt afraid in
case Conor saw them. 'I—I mustn't spend any time with
you, Geoff,' she said huskily, studying him. 'It might
make you think I—I was returning your feelings. I
mean—you kissed me the other day and I——'

'Oh, don't worry!' he said, frowning. 'It was just an
impulse! Nothing much behind it!'

She watched him, biting her lip.

'Really,' he assured her with a light smile, 'just one
of those things. A sunny day, a pretty girl...' He shrugged
slender shoulders. 'I'm a man. I'm as prey to these things
as the next guy.'

Diana smiled slightly, and looked away. 'OK. That
sounds fair enough.' Her eyes darted to the ballroom as
she heard Conor talking. 'Let's walk, then...' And she
took his arm as she dragged him across the lawns at a
very brisk pace, looking over her shoulder as she did in
case Conor saw them.

'Hey...!' Geoff was laughing as they almost ran across
the pebble-strewn path that led round to the front drive.
'For a girl who's not interested, you have a funny way
of showing it!'

'What?' She stared, then took her hand from his arm,
flushing. 'Sorry, I just wanted to...to get away from
the château. I'm sick of it, to be honest...'

'Oh?' His pale brows lifted. 'That's a coincidence. So
am I.'

She shrugged lightly. 'We've been working intensively
here for a week. It's only natural.' The warm breeze blew
gently through the nearby rose bushes, sending sweet
scent into her nostrils.

'Well——' he spread his hands '—why don't we really
get away? I mean—you've got the afternoon off, haven't
you? We could go into town, have a glass of anisette at
a café, feel *très Francais*...watch the old men playing
boules...'

Diana shook her head even though she was deeply
tempted to escape the château. 'I don't think so.'

'Oh, go on!' he wheedled, smiling. 'I can see you want to! Your eyes have lit up and you've got a bit of colour back into your cheeks!'

She dimpled, lowering her lashes. 'It would be nice...'

'Right,' he said firmly, 'then we'll go. Silly to stay here when you're not needed.'

Diana looked into his eyes with a serious, silent expression and thought, that's right. I'm not needed. That's exactly what's wrong. Conor doesn't need me and he never did. He only ever wanted to make love to me until he was bored with me: and what woman would want that?

'All right,' she said slowly, nodding. 'Let's go.'

The town square was scented with Frenchness. The hot afternoon sun blazed through the leaves of the trees to dapple the dusty ground with light and shade. A group of old men played boules near by, the clink of steel against steel mingling with their Gallic laughter and conversation. It was a Sunday, and everyone was at leisure, the town cafés crowded with people drinking cool drinks or espresso coffee and watching life go past at its tranquil, very summery and very French pace.

'Slade was a tyrant this morning, wasn't he?' Geoff said as their drinks arrived. 'I felt so sorry for you, having to suffer his slings and arrows.'

Diana toyed with her glass of anisette. 'He was in a bad temper.'

'He often is,' drawled Geoff, 'but let's hope Talia Hite cheers him up.'

'Talia Hite?' Diana looked up sharply.

'Yes, she's arriving this afternoon—didn't you know?'

White, Diana shook her head. 'I'd forgotten,' she said stiffly, jealousy shooting through her as she remembered Conor telling her about his love-affair with the notorious actress. How could she have forgotten that Talia was arriving today?

'And if anyone can soothe the savage beast,' Geoff said wryly, 'it's Talia Hite.'

Dry-mouthed, shot through with jealousy, Diana managed to say, 'Didn't they have an...an affair of some kind?'

'On the set of *The Derringer*.' Geoff nodded. 'I was working on it, too. Talia was playing the lead, of course. A vamp.'

'What else?' Diana said thickly.

'Oh, she was sensational, too!' Geoff laughed, shaking his head. 'Her usual style—drooping eyelids, red lips, clinging black dresses and more sex appeal than a loaded gun.'

'How nice,' Diana said tightly.

'So...' Geoff was watching her with those pale blue eyes '...once Talia arrives, Conor should stop hounding you.'

She swallowed on a dry throat. 'I...I suppose so.'

Geoff's hand closed slowly over hers on the table. 'And if he does stop hounding you, you might be relaxed enough to consent to an evening out with me.'

Diana looked at him through her dark glasses and said huskily, 'That's very kind of you, Geoff, but I——'

'Don't say but,' he drawled softly, smiling at her. 'And certainly don't say kind!'

Diana smiled slowly. 'Look—I do appreciate your invitation——'

'Then accept it. What harm can it do?'

That was a very good point, and Diana considered it in silence as she studied him.

'It is Slade, isn't it?' Geoff said suddenly, pale brows drawn in a frown. 'I've been wondering if there was anything between you. Now I'm beginning to be sure.'

'Well,' she said quickly, 'as I told you, we did know each other before we made the film.'

'And how well did you know each other?' His brows rose. 'As well as he knew Talia?'

This time the jealousy was more than she could bear, and her face ran with hot angry colour, her mouth tightening as she looked at Geoff in silence, hating herself for being such a fool as to even care what Conor Slade did.

'Ah...' Geoff said, softly, eyes flickering over her face. 'I see.'

'No,' she said at once, 'you don't see. But——' She held his hand across the table, and said urgently, 'But I can't tell you, Geoff. I—I don't know you well enough yet, and it is so very personal.'

He nodded. 'It was a romantic involvement, then?'

She bent her head, saying huskily, 'In a way. But—but it didn't last long. And it was such a long time ago...'

Geoff was silent for a moment, then said gently, 'Well—it all sounds very much in the past, then, doesn't it? And you know the best place for the past, don't you?'

Diana shrugged slim shoulders in the sunshine.

'The past,' Geoff said with a smile. 'Just cut it off and let it go. Simple as that.'

She suddenly shivered as though a ghost had walked over her grave, and all she could see in her mind were the dark Celtic mountains of Connemara and the blood-red sky above.

'So!' Geoff grinned at her. 'Can I put you down in my Filofax for dinner tomorrow night?'

Diana studied him for a long moment, thinking of Talia Hite arriving this afternoon, and Conor's old love-affair with her starting up again, and suddenly she felt such a colossal fool. I'm just another old love-affair to him, she thought furiously. Just a pretty girl to pass the time with until the next one arrives.

'Yes!' she said suddenly to Geoff, her eyes angry. 'Yes, I'd love to have dinner with you tomorrow night!'

The château was as dustily beautiful as ever, and the sun blazed down on its tryptych and its bleached altar as Geoff drove up the tree-lined drive in his red Renault Fuego.

'That must be Talia's car,' drawled Geoff, gesturing to the long black Cadillac limousine with French number-plates parked outside the château doors, a tall, enigmatic chauffeur standing beside it in black peaked-cap uniform, holding a white dog on a lead.

'And Talia's dog,' Diana said, staring at the magnificent highly strung, long-nosed creature as it strained at the leash and shook with overbred nerves. 'What is it?'

'A borzoi,' said Geoff, parking behind the Cadillac. 'Russian hunting hound. The Czars used them. Fantastic, aren't they?'

'Ravishing...' Diana said, getting out of the car, feeling intensely ordinary and inferior as she walked slowly past the symbols of Talia Hite's legend.

The great hall was deserted, the chandelier swaying softly in the warm breeze. Music echoed down the marble corridors from the ballroom, and Diana frowned, listening to the pain-filled voice, the angry guitar and the vibrant piano.

'What on earth...?' she said, turning to Geoff.

'Talia Hite has arrived!' drawled Geoff, hands on hips. 'That's Russsorgsky; the Russian protest singer. She plays him constantly. Part of her image.'

'But why should she be playing it here?'

'Let's go and find out, shall we?' Geoff said with a laugh, and took her hand. 'Come on! It sounds like quite a party!'

The great Louis XV clock in the ballroom was chiming a pure gold six as they entered, and what met their eyes made Diana catch her breath and freeze on the spot, white with jealousy, pain and rage.

Talia Hite was dancing in the centre of the ballroom, a red rose between her teeth, long black hair swinging like silk as she spun like a gypsy in black, clinging black, the kind of black that drove men mad, her white breasts rising and falling with exertion as her green eyes flashed at Conor Slade and the music of Russorgsky filled the ballroom with vibrant emotion.

'Isn't she something?' Geoff whispered in Diana's ear.

'She certainly is...' Diana breathed thickly, rooted to the spot, as mesmerised by the beautiful black-haired witch as everyone else in the room was, all staring in silence as Talia danced like Salome for Conor Slade: her warrior king, her Herod... her lover.

The jealousy was so severe that Diana could not move.
It seemed to have flooded her bloodstream like a drug,
and was now beginning to prickle along her skin from
the inside as though a thousand tiny needles were trying
to get out.

How could Conor just stand there watching her like
that? Watching her through his lids with such obvious
interest? Such arousal... such cool, controlled arousal,
as though he knew that—as soon as the dance was over—
Talia would be his to do with as he wished.

The hatred flashed from her blue eyes, and at that
moment Conor slowly, deliberately flicked his gaze to
meet hers.

He saw it, damn him! He saw the jealousy she could
not hide and his hard mouth twisted with cynical triumph
as he looked back at Talia and deliberately allowed his
gaze to rove over her body as it twisted and flashed before
him.

Diana turned on her heel and walked out, shaking.

I'm not in love with him! she told herself fiercely as
she ran down the marble corridor. I'm not! I wouldn't
be such a fool! I couldn't love a man like that!

She was running up the stairs, running to her bedroom,
and as she locked her door behind her she found herself
breathing harshly, tears stinging her eyes as she struggled
to remain calm.

It was all just a game! she realised, and stumbled
across the bedroom to her balcony, leaning on the rail,
breathing in great gulps of warm evening air and staring
at the fierce sunlight beyond the acres and acres of
bleached land.

He only wanted a woman in his arms, in his bed, she
realised with appalled understanding. That was all it was.
All that stuff about our being twin souls, about how he
couldn't live without me because we were one and the
same... it was all just rubbish!

It was just a line and I bought it!

'Oh, God!' she whispered, closing her eyes on fresh
tears. 'What have I done...?'

Dinner was at eight that night, and Diana dressed for it very carefully indeed. With Talia Hite at the table, she would have to feel as secure in herself as a woman as it was possible for her to feel.

She chose a dark blue silk strapless dress. It fitted her slender curves like a glove, and her heart thumped as she zipped it up, feeling very daring indeed, for, although the hem was at knee level, there were splits at both sides of the skirt, making it almost like a Chinese girl's cheung-san.

Did she dare wear it? That was the question. She bit her lip, feeling very unsure of herself. Then she remembered Talia Hite and decided to brave it, regardless. Brushing her blonde hair, she suddenly wished it was dark again... long, thick and glossy black. The silver earrings she wore would have looked better against black hair, and as she turned her head the earrings jangled like gypsy bells.

When she arrived downstairs, she was pleased to hear no Russian music, and enjoyed the silence as she walked down the corridor towards the dining-room.

Talia Hite was holding court at the dinner table. Everyone had dressed for dinner. The male crew members, all in suits and with well-brushed hair, were vying for her attention while Conor Slade, damn him, sat back at the head of the table, watching Talia through those heavy-lidded eyes.

'Ah,' Conor drawled as he saw Diana at the doorway, 'here's your co-star, Talia. Miss Diana Sullivan!'

All heads turned to look at Diana, and she squirmed inside as she forced herself to walk forwards to Talia Hite, who was watching her with narrowed green eyes, her gaze flicking over Diana as though she were an unwanted autograph-hunter.

'I'm pleased to meet you, Miss Hite!' Diana said huskily, her pride and her manners warring, and her manners winning as she extended a slim pale hand. 'I've seen all your films, and I'm looking forward to working with you.'

Talia regarded her hand with an icy smile, then extended her very long, red-taloned fingers and shook her hand coolly, saying in that throaty voice, 'Dahlink, forgive me, but I haven't seen any of your vork. I'm sure you're very good, though, or you vould hardly be starring vith me.'

Conor was watching her face, and Diana knew she had turned red after that very politely delivered insult.

'And, of course,' Talia said with a red-lipped smile, 'you're such a good foil for me. So small and blonde and...' her black lashes flickered '...innocent.'

Diana suddenly had a strong urge to pour something over the woman's head.

Talia turned to Conor with a smile. 'Such a masterstroke to unite us in this film!' she drawled, placing her red-taloned hand on his dark sleeve. 'Only you, Conor, my love, could have thought of it!'

'I do my best,' Conor replied, flicking his cool gaze to Diana's face.

'Oh, dahlink...' murmured Talia with a very hot look. 'I know!'

There was a brief silence. Diana walked stiffly to one of the few spare seats and sank down on to it, trembling, so sick with jealousy that she felt as though she'd just been hit in the solar plexus by a ten-ton sledge-hammer.

'Isn't she unspeakable?' drawled Georgina beside her in an inaudible whisper. 'She'll make a great witch!'

Diana looked up at her, blue eyes filled with jealousy. 'Her role isn't very big, is it?' she asked under her breath. 'I mean—she won't be around for very long, will she?'

Georgina's green eyes were only too understanding. 'Not as long as you, darling.' She patted her hand. 'Rest assured of that.'

'Playing Chinese whispers, Georgina?' Conor's cool voice drawled from the head of the table and both Diana and Georgina looked at him sharply.

'Absolutely, darling!' trilled Georgina with a bright laugh. 'But we couldn't possibly let you in on the secret, because we were whispering about you!'

Diana bent her head, mortified, and stared at her salade niçoise.

'Really?' Conor said, eyes narrowing on Diana's averted face. 'I suppose it——' He broke off sharply as Geoff sauntered into the room, walked straight towards Diana, bent his head and murmured something inaudible in her ear before taking the seat beside her. 'Good evening, Mr Hastings!' Conor said tightly, watching him. 'As you can see, Miss Hite has arrived, and, as her coach, you should have presented yourself to her sooner!'

Geoff stiffened, casting a quick glance at Diana before turning to Conor and saying, 'I'm sorry, Mr Slade. I was in town when Miss Hite arrived and——'

'In town?' Conor frowned, eyes narrowing.

He nodded, saying lightly, 'With Miss Sullivan. We went for a drink in the square. We forgot the time.'

Conor's blue eyes focused sharply on Diana's flushed face and she saw the anger flash in them, saw his mouth tighten with grim condemnation, and knew exactly what he was thinking.

'Don't vorry, dahlink,' Talia was drawling lazily, 'the last thing I vant tonight is to rehearse. Geoff can come to me tomorrow in my trailer.'

Conor said nothing, his mouth hard with anger as he stared at Diana.

'And, besides,' Talia placed a red-taloned hand on Conor's dark sleeve again, 'I'd love to go to the square myself...later...vith you...' Her red lips twisted as she added, 'Dahlink!'

Diana quickly looked away, her face tight with jealousy as she heard Conor drawl in reply, 'We'll go after dinner.'

Diana picked up her wine glass with a trembling hand. She had to be strong, and she had to make it look as though she didn't care two hoots whether Conor started up his old love-affair or not. But it was so very, very hard.

'Oh, God,' drawled Geoff beside her with a smile, 'not salade niçoise again!'

Diana turned with a grateful smile, and started to talk to him. She managed to keep up her brave front all through dinner, managed to ignore Conor and Talia publicly, while privately hearing every single word they said to each other.

'What are you doing after dinner?' Geoff asked her as the caterers cleared their plates away.

'I don't know...' Diana said huskily, shooting a glance to Conor at the head of the table and burning inside as she watched him kiss Talia Hite's hand.

'I'm having a game of cards with the boys,' Geoff told her. 'Do you play?'

'Which game?' Diana asked, aware out of the corner of her eye that Talia was feeding Conor a wafer-thin sliver of chocolate.

'Three-card brag,' Geoff said, smiling. 'For centimes.'

She gave a tense laugh. 'The stakes are high, then!'

'Dahlink,' drawled Talia's throaty voice as she slid the last piece of chocolate into Conor's mouth with her long fingers, 'if there vere grapes on the table, I vould peel zem for you...'

Diana's mouth trembled with jealousy. The stakes were as high as they could get. How could Conor sit there allowing that woman to blatantly seduce him in front of her? After everything he'd said...all his prot- estations about how they were as one? She could have killed him. She could have stood up with a scream and swept all the crockery off the table, and thrown the cream over Talia Hite's beautiful, seductive head.

After dinner she went into the games-room with Geoff and the boys. It was a large room at the front of the château with green baize tables, low lights, and a drinks cabinet in the corner.

'OK!' Geoff was saying as he shuffled. 'Cool Hand Geoff is here! Let's see the colour of your money...centimes on the table!'

'Hit me, Martini, hit me!' laughed the cameraman.

'First one out is whisky-whalla!' said the best-boy.

Outside, Diana heard the slam of car doors. Dry- mouthed, she got to her feet, saying, 'I'll get the whisky,' and walked quickly to the windows, pulling back the dark green curtain to stare out, heart thudding, at the drive.

Conor's steel-blue Citroën was close by. Talia was in the passenger-seat, running a hand through Conor's thick black hair as she whispered something intimately in his ear.

Jealousy shot through her, making her blood throb and her stomach clench with rage and pain. The Citroën engine flared, dust kicked up as the wheels spun, and she stood at the window, white-faced, watching Conor and Talia roar away down the drive in a cloud of dust.

'Diana?' Geoff's voice floated to her suddenly. 'Are you OK?'

She turned, stiffening, struggling to mask the fierce jealousy in her eyes as she said with a tight smile, 'Yes, I'm fine! Now—what did you want, boys? Whisky...?'

The game went on, seemingly, forever. Diana sat at the table, playing the occasional hand, struggling to keep her mind off Conor and Talia and failing.

I was just another ex-mistress, she kept thinking; and it was a self-torturing thought that she could not stop. No matter what she did, how hard she tried not to care, it kept leaping back at her like a bullet between the eyes: just another ex-mistress...

'I'm out,' the cameraman sighed, throwing in his hand.

'Raise you twenty,' said Geoff, grinning at the sound-engineer.

The sound-engineer threw forty centimes in. 'I'll see you.'

Geoff grinned and laid down his hand with flair. 'Three aces!'

Everyone groaned with disgust.

'Thank you, boys!' Geoff was laughing, claiming his winnings. 'Candy from babies!' He raised pale brows. 'Another hand?'

'No, it's ten-thirty,' said the cameraman, 'and we've got a five a.m. wake-up call. Goodnight!'

'I'd better be going to bed, too,' Diana said huskily, getting up from the table. 'I'm rather tired...'

Geoff stood up as the others filed out of the room. 'Let me clear this away, then I'll see you to your room.'

'No,' Diana said at once, shaking her head as she moved away, 'I—I'm really exhausted, Geoff. I-I'll see you in the morning...' She escaped quickly and went up to her room.

Of course; Conor was not back. Diana would have heard the car, and as she closed her bedroom door she finally allowed herself the luxury of seething inside with a jealousy she had not known she was capable of feeling.

The pain was bad enough. But the madness of jealousy was intolerable, and she hated herself for the violence of it, hated herself for feeling so betrayed, so humiliated, so possessive.

Possessive! What right did she have to feel so possessive about Conor? Hadn't she left him? Denied for years that she felt anything for him? And yet now—look at her! Trembling with rage and jealousy and pain like a woman scorned in the grip of a powerful obsession!

Quickly, she got undressed and got into bed. But she couldn't sleep. She had known she wouldn't sleep, wouldn't rest until Conor was back. What if he made love to Talia tonight? Oh, God, the jealousy was like fire in her stomach and she twisted and turned, burning up.

She got up, walked across the room to her balcony, opened the doors and went out into the moonlit night. Crickets chirped loudly all around her. The moon hung like a silver mandala in the night sky.

I'm not going to sleep until he gets back, she realised, and I'll have to accept it. Gritting her teeth, she got a chair and sat down on it, on the balcony, to begin her obsessive vigil.

At half-past eleven, she heard the car. Her heart thundered with jealous rage as she sat, silent and moonstruck in her white négligé, listening as the engine cut out.

It was twenty minutes later that Conor returned to his room.

Diana sat, white and silent, as her unfaithful lover closed his bedroom door and walked across the room to open the balcony doors.

She stiffened in alarm, but could not move, and as Conor stepped out on to his balcony she stared at him in paralysed terror, her face white with shock.

In the moonlit night, Conor turned his head and saw her.

The crickets chirped.

The air was warm.

There was lipstick on his scarred cheek.

'What are you doing?' he asked. 'Why are you still up?'

Diana stared at the lipstick on his cheek and could not reply.

'You realise it's almost midnight?' Conor said flatly. 'You have to be up at——'

'Dawn,' she said thickly. 'I know. I just . . . couldn't sleep.' Her face flushed and she looked at the silver moon glowing above them both, saying, 'It must be the moon. It's full tonight, isn't it?'

Conor's gaze flicked up to it. 'About as full as it could get.'

Diana's eyes moved over his profile as he studied the moon, and she felt so much pain just looking at him and imagining Talia Hite pressing her red lips against his hard cheekbone.

'I wonder how it felt,' Conor said coolly, 'to walk on it.' He turned, looking at her with those passionate eyes. 'To be Neil Armstrong . . . the first man on the moon. I wanted to be an astronaut when I was a little boy.'

Diana looked at him and felt waves of jealous rage. 'Did you?' she asked bitterly, hating him.

'I like excitement,' Conor said, looking at the moon, 'adventure, danger . . .' he turned and met her blue gaze '. . . anything that stirs up the blood and makes me feel alive.'

'Like Talia Hite?' Diana said in a low, angry voice.

His black lashes flickered. 'Talia . . . ?'

'Yes,' Diana said tightly, 'Talia Hite! Russian accent, borzoi and black Cadillac! You remember her, Conor! She left her lips all over your face!'

She got to her feet, shaking, and the chair fell over with a crash as she turned and stormed into her room.

CHAPTER SEVEN

CONOR landed on Diana's balcony with a perfectly executed leap, sprang to his feet and stood framed in the doorway, the moonlight his only illumination. Diana turned, catching her breath in the darkness of her bedroom. Shaking with jealous fury, she could only stand and stare at him, and feel a thrill of hope that he had followed her after that outburst of possessive rage from her.

'Say that again!' he demanded under his breath, watching her.

Diana laughed angrily. 'I don't think I will, Conor! It would be bad for your ego, and we both know how big that is! After all—Talia Hite has been feeding it all night!'

His eyes narrowed. 'What the hell is that supposed to mean?'

'Dahlink!' Diana mimicked, blue eyes flashing with fury. 'If there vere grapes on the table, I vould peel zem for you!'

Conor laughed under his breath. 'So that's it!' he said softly, eyes glittering in the darkness. 'You're jealous!'

'I am not jealous!' she denied hotly, flushing scarlet.

'Don't deny it, my love!' he said under his breath, walking towards her, magnificent in black evening trousers, white shirt unbuttoned at the throat, black tie hanging loose around his collar. 'I know you better than you think!'

'I felt embarrassed for you!' Diana flung angrily. 'And for her! Feeding you chocolates at the dinner-table and offering her wrist for a kiss! I'm surprised she didn't just kneel at your feet on a silk cushion and address you as master!' She was shocked by herself, appalled at the jealousy spilling out of her like a haemorrhage, but she couldn't stop herself, couldn't dam it up and keep it out of sight, keep her dignity, her self-esteem, her self-respect in his eyes.

'Oh, it's all coming out now!' Conor drawled, stopping in front of her, a smile of pure triumph on his hard mouth as he took her chin in one hand. 'Carry on, darling! I always wondered what it would be like to see you jealous, and now I know!'

'I told you!' she said fiercely, jerking her chin out of his grasp. 'I'm not jealous! Just embarrassed for you! I've never seen such a display of——'

'You're beautiful!' he said on a tense, excited whisper. 'Your eyes are flashing like fire!'

'Men are such fools!' she said hoarsely. 'But I thought you were different, Conor! Imagine falling for that act of hers! Peel you grapes indeed! I've never seen such——'

'Maybe I find her irresistible,' he said under his breath. 'Has that ever occurred to you?'

She caught her breath, fury in her eyes.

'Maybe I never got her out of my mind!' Conor's eyes glittered.

The pain hit her like a steam-train. 'I don't doubt it! Not a bit, Conor! I'm sure you've just been waiting for her to arrive—haven't you? And this little—game you've been playing with me was always just that! A game!'

He watched her, breathing heavily, his eyes glittering over her. 'Maybe it was...'

'And the game begins again with Talia!' she said hoarsely. 'I bet you can't wait to go to bed with her!'

He smiled slowly. 'Maybe I already have!'

There was an electric silence. In the darkness, her eyes blazed at him with a thousand different emotions, and the betrayal cut so deep, the jealousy so violent, and the sense of possession filled her with rage.

'You bastard!' With a hoarse cry she launched herself at him, hitting him on the shoulders, the chest, blind with emotion as she fought bitterly, her hands slapping his face and trying to scratch him.

Conor struggled to control her. Thick sounds of rage came from both their throats, and they were fighting in bitter silence, skin and bone hitting the only sound in the dark bedroom.

He got her wrists in a biting grip. In a split second his arms were around her and as his hard mouth came down over hers she gave a low sound of angry pleasure.

Suddenly, they were clinging together, their mouths passionate as they kissed, and Diana was crushed against his hard body, her heart racing as she thrust her fingers into his hair, harsh sounds of pleasure coming from both of them as the kiss grew more wildly demanding.

His strong hands were running over her body and she was gasping, her head back to receive his kiss, blood throbbing through her body, pressing against him in blind need, her limbs like liquid fire.

When his strong hand closed over her breast and stroked her erect nipple through the diaphanous négligé Diana almost fainted with hot desire, breathing hoarsely even as she moaned and whispered, 'Oh, yes...yes...!'

'I'll have you now!' Conor said thickly, his heart thundering in his hard chest. 'I'll have you like this...on fire or not at all!' He swept her into his strong arms, carrying her to the bed, laying her down on it and joining her with a thick sound of excitement as his mouth closed over hers again.

Diana twisted against him on the bed, moaning as he slid one hand on to her slim thigh, pushing the négligé slowly higher, and her quick restless gasps of excitement inflamed him further, made him grind his teeth as he bent his head, tugged the garment roughly aside and closed his hard hot mouth over her bare breast, sucking hungrily as she thrust her hands into his black hair.

She felt helplessly joined with him. They were as one, now, tonight, at this moment, their bodies consumed by the same fire as they twisted together on the bed and Conor shed his shirt, coming back to her to lift her head and press her hot mouth against his bare chest, biting out, 'Yes . . . ! Do it . . . !' and Diana slid passionate kisses over his tanned flesh, her tongue curling in the thick black hairs of his chest while Conor's heart thundered like a rocket and his hands thrust into her hair while he breathed harshly.

'You want me!' Conor said thickly, pushing her back against the pillows, both semi-nude now, their limbs moving together as though they were one person with four arms and legs, some hot-blooded writhing creature caught in the moonlit four-poster bed in frenzy. 'You want me and now you're going to tell me or I'll kill you, Diana! I swear I'll kill you unless I hear it from your lips!'

'Go to hell!' Diana said hoarsely, blue eyes bright with pain as she denied him. 'You've just made love to another woman! Go to her! I'm sure *she'll* tell you!'

His eyes blazed. 'You know damn well I only said that to provoke you!'

'Liar!' she said fiercely. 'I can smell her scent on your throat and see her lipstick on your cheek!'

'Don't be so ridiculous!' he bit out. 'I admit she kissed me but you must know it went no further than that!'

'I don't know anything of the sort!'

'Then why are you making love to me like a wildcat?' he asked thickly, his hand shaking on her breast as he cupped it. 'Oh, God, you drive me insane, Diana . . . you're even more passionate than you were when——'

'I did it because I was so angry I wanted to kill you!' Diana cried. 'But I'm not strong enough to kill you so I decided to . . . to . . .' She broke off lamely, breathing erratically, suddenly aware of just how far she had gone and feeling horrified by the danger she was now in.

'To make love to me instead?' he asked deeply.

'Yes!' Diana said hoarsely. 'It just exploded in me!'

Their eyes met as they lay in the tangled sheets, clothes pushed aside, bodies damp with sweat and eyes filled with passion.

Conor stroked her hair, his heart thudding violently as he said, 'But don't you see how completely perfect that is?'

'I feel like an animal!' she whispered in paroxysms of guilt and shame. 'And you deliberately provoked that in me!'

'To make you see how you really felt about me, Diana,' he said deeply, watching her closely. 'And I think it worked—don't you?'

Her mouth trembled. 'It made me see quite what a ruthless, immoral bastard you are, Conor! You made love to that—that witch, and then you came here to taunt me with——'

'No,' he said at once, shaking his head. 'I——'

'Just to get what you wanted!' she cut in, tears burning her eyes. 'I've never seen such manipulation! My God, you make Machiavelli look like a saint!'

'I shouldn't have done it,' Conor said harshly, 'but I had to do something! Last night I thought we'd got through all this. I thought we'd reached an understanding, and that sooner or later——'

'This would happen?' she asked bitterly.

He studied her for a second, then replied, 'Among other things, yes.'

'And you think I should be willing to fulfil that fond hope, Conor?' she asked huskily, the tears stinging her eyes so badly she couldn't see. 'I hate to disillusion you, but it's never going to happen.'

'But it is happening,' he said flatly, his blue eyes very dark as they pierced hers. 'It's happening now and you were with me all the way!'

Hot colour burned her face with shame. 'It was a moment's folly. That's all. I've burnt out all the anger I felt—now I just feel disgust, Conor, and——'

'Disgust?' he bit out, shaking, staring at her in disbelief.

She almost flinched, but forced herself to stand her ground. 'Yes! What else can I feel?'

He studied her for a long moment in silence, his mouth shaking. Diana watched his face in the darkness, and, as those blue eyes glittered down at her, as the tousled black hair fell forwards slightly into his eyes, as he raked it back impatiently with one strong, arrogant hand, she realised she was in love with him.

I'm in love, she thought, her heart stopping. All respiration stopped. She felt as though she'd been spun out of time to face her feelings, and in that split second she saw her life flash before her eyes as though she were a woman drowning.

I've always loved him, she realised dumbly. Always...

'All right!' Conor's harsh voice brought her back to reality with a thud. 'Lie there in your lonely bed, you little bitch! Lie here with your dyed-blonde hair and your empty life and your jealousy and tell yourself you don't love me, don't want me!' He pushed her away roughly, getting to his feet, breathing harshly as he stared down at her white, tortured face, raked a hand through his black hair and said bitingly, 'I'll take your advice and go to Talia! I'm sure the very last thing she would feel if I made love to her is disgust!' He turned on his heel and slammed out of the room.

Diana couldn't move. She felt as though her whole body was in pain. It hurt to breathe, and she didn't know how it would feel if she moved, so she just lay there, white and rigid, fighting the waves of pain that washed through her.

I fell in love with him the first moment I saw him. Of course, it hadn't been obvious to her then. Just a sudden violent attraction, the feeling of a channel opening up between two people as they had looked into each other's eyes in a hail of glass.

Never told him, she thought, dashing the tears away. Never really knew it myself. Diana sprawled across the pillows, eyes and cheeks wet with salty tears. I should have told him when we were married, then he would have known how I felt, and never put me through this agony...

He'd been playing with her heart out of pity. He felt sorry for her because she was still alone, still lonely. God, that stung! And to see him give up out of boredom and turn his attentions towards Talia stung even more. How jealousy burnt!

She couldn't sleep, just lay there in agony, her mind revolving on the betrayal. As dawn broke, she began to fall asleep, and welcomed the oblivion.

The wake-up call brought her back to the real world as she replaced the receiver and remembered everything that had happened last night. She told herself to get on with her work and forget Conor, but she knew that that would be impossible. If she hadn't stopped loving him in six years, why should she stop now?

Diana's eyes were swollen and raw. Her skin was ashen. She hid behind a pair of dark glasses and went down to breakfast in a dark blue sun-dress.

Everyone was downstairs, milling about in a subdued, five o'clock-in-the-morning sort of way.

Talia Hite swept into the dining-room fully made-up, exuding glamour, and casting a cool, patronising look at Diana from beneath her heavy eyelids.

'Dahlink,' she purred, 'you look like death! Vot happened?'

'I couldn't sleep,' Diana managed to say through her jealousy.

'I bet you're hiding black circles behind those dark glasses,' drawled Talia, her green eyes glittering with cat-like malice. 'Conor will be very cross viz you. He's already vorried about your acting, dahlink. He told me last night.'

Diana stared at her, mouth trembling, unable to speak.

'He told me a lot of things last night,' Talia purred, sipping black coffee, red mouth curving. 'Ve stayed out quite late, you know...'

After breakfast, Diana boarded the minibus to go to the location shoot, and, although she huddled at the back in dark glasses, blue sun-dress and a straw sun-hat, Georgina spotted her at once and came sailing down the aisle towards her with a bright smile, her purple dress splendid on her voluptuous figure.

'You're very jumpy today,' Georgina observed, sitting beside her as the minibus started up and they pulled away. 'Is anything wrong?'

'No,' Diana said huskily, 'nothing.'

'Rather white, too,' Georgina continued. 'Didn't you sleep?'

'I—I always have trouble sleeping when it's a full moon.'

'Ah,' Georgina said softly, 'it was the moon, then? Not the man?'

Diana's mouth trembled and she looked down at her hands, swallowing to try and stop the tears that sprang suddenly to her eyes, glad of the sanctuary of dark glasses.

'Conor's in a frightful temper this morning,' Georgina said lightly as they rattled across a field in the bus. 'You should have seen him! Biting people's heads off, stamping around like a bull in an arena...wearing a very fetching pair of dark glasses, too!'

Diana stared at her, hope springing like wildfire in her heart. Was it possible, just possible that Conor had meant what he'd said? Right from the start?

The bus bumped to a standstill in the dawn-dewed field. The first person she saw was Conor, and her heart skidded to a standstill as she stopped dead, staring up into that powerful face, his eyes shielded, as Georgina had said, by dark glasses.

'Conor!' Diana said huskily, feeling suddenly tongue-tied. 'I—I'm glad I've run into you so quickly. I—I just wanted to——'

'I'm sorry, I don't have time for a chat!' Conor said tightly, brushing past her to the minibus driver. 'Did you bring the best-boy? Well, damn it, where is he? He should have been here with us an hour ago!' He slammed his hand on the side of the bus. 'Well, get back over there and drag him here! Tell him I'll have his head on a plate if he does this once more!'

Diana hovered behind him, heart thudding too fast, and when he turned round she said, 'I don't suppose you could spare a minute during filming? Just—just for a quick word.'

His mouth tightened. 'I doubt it.'

'But Conor, I must talk to you!' she said urgently, and the tone of her voice stopped him in his tracks. He really did look gorgeous today. The blue jeans, white shirt and black open waistcoat made him look dangerously sexy, his black hair tousled as he ran a hand through it.

'Well?' he said flatly, hands on hips. 'What is it?'

Diana glanced self-consciously around. 'Not in front of all these people...'

He pulled his dark glasses off, and she saw with a sinking heart that his blue eyes had no circles under them, that he looked fresh and clean-shaven and very much in control of his heart.

'Look,' he said tightly, 'I'm pushed for time. What is it? Costume gone astray? Row with the make-up girls? What?'

She stared at him, the colour draining from her face as she realised how completely she had almost made a fool of herself. He didn't love her. He probably hadn't thought twice about that row last night. He'd probably just gone to bed, telling himself he would take Talia instead.

'Nothing,' she said hoarsely, backing away from him, shaking her head. 'It—it was nothing!' She turned and ran towards her trailer, tears stinging her eyes, and did not know he watched her with an intent frown as she went.

Filming was a tension-ridden experience. Conor alternately snapped at her and gave impatient sighs. She felt hopelessly inept, and actually forgot her lines on one occasion.

'Diana,' Conor said tightly through the loudspeaker after the eleventh take, 'the line is: "Should the Royal House of Sarcaronne ever stand in peril."'

'I know,' she said with intense frustration, aware of Talia Hite smirking like mad beside her. 'I just keep

getting tripped up by the words. Can't you rearrange
them or something?'

'No,' Conor replied, 'but we can always write them
on a card for you.'

Diana was so nervous by this time that she fluffed the
line even when it was written in big red letters on a board
to her right.

'Cut!' Conor shouted, and threw down the loudspeaker. 'Fifteen minutes, everybody! Diana—not you!
Come over here. I want a word with you!'

It was an authoritative summons. Diana went over to
him, trembling, aware that she felt as though she were
being hauled in front of the headmaster for some mis-
demeanour, and resenting that.

'All right!' Conor said under his breath, hands on
hips. 'What is this—a deliberate campaign?'

She stared at him angrily. 'Don't be so ludicrous! I
just can't say the words! Mental block of some sort—it
happens!'

'Diana,' he said with infinite patience, 'that is not a
difficult line. I agree, it's a little old-fashioned, but you're
reading it from an ancient manuscript, for God's sake!
It's supposed to be old-fashioned!'

'I know,' she said huskily, lowering her lashes, 'and
I'm sorry. Maybe I'll get it right next time.'

He studied her in silence for a moment, then he asked
shrewdly, 'Is it something personal?'

She looked up warily.

'The mental blockage,' Conor said under his breath,
blue eyes intent. 'Is it caused by personal problems?'

Diana gave a husky laugh. 'How very professional you
sound...anyone would think you had nothing to do with
it!'

'Me?' He stared, then his hands shot out and caught
her shoulders as he asked roughly, 'It's me? It's because
of last night?'

'Please let go!' Diana said thickly, her heart thudding
like mad. 'You're hurting——'

'Diana, you must tell me!' he said urgently. 'If what happened last night has thrown you off balance, then you have to tell me.'

She looked at him bitterly, and asked, 'Made love to Talia yet?'

There was a long silence. They looked into one another's eyes, and Conor's hands were motionless on her shoulders as the sun beat down on them and she felt the wrench of unrequited love deep in her soul.

'I'm sorry,' she murmured, pride coming to her rescue, 'I had no right to say that. It's none of my business, after all, and——'

'Of course it's your business!' he said deeply. 'It's everything to do with you, you little fool!'

She looked up, catching her breath.

'Don't you see?' Conor said on a harsh sigh. 'If you're as insanely jealous of her as I think you are——'

'I've told you!' she said tightly, wriggling suddenly to escape those strong fingers. 'I'm not jealous of her and I never have been! I just dislike her personally! It's perfectly natural. She's not everybody's cup of tea. There's no law that says I have to——'

'Don't lie to me!' he said furiously, blue eyes flaring with sudden passion. 'Don't you see I *want* you to be jealous? If you really don't want me, you'll be indifferent to Talia, but if you——'

'The whole world doesn't revolve around you, Conor!' she said hoarsely, her face flaming with hot colour. 'And my professional dislike of Talia has nothing, nothing and *nothing* to do with you!' She wrenched herself out of his grasp, turned and ran from him before he could stop her.

Reaching the caterers' trailer, Diana leaned weakly against the burning hot metal, her heart thudding and her skin flushed. The scent of lunch being cooked was almost enough to deprive her of her breakfast.

Turning, she looked back at Conor, hating him, thinking of what he had just said and feeling incredulous that any man could have the sheer inhumanity to say it!

'If you're as insanely jealous as I think you are...' he had said, and, my God, he deserved the award for cruelty to dumb blondes for that one! She felt like a dumb blonde right now: she really did. What a fool, she berated herself, what an almighty fool! All he wanted was a mistress, and here she was building it up into the love-affair of the century!

'Had a little row with dahlink Conor?' drawled a throaty voice beside her, and Diana looked up, stiffening, as Talia Hite swayed to a standstill beside her.

'Miss Hite...' Diana said, playing for time, her face flushing crimson as she looked at that beautiful face and thought: you made love to my husband!

'Zat was quite something, dahlink!' Talia purred, red lips curving. 'Next time you better know your lines, properly, hmm? Or zat savage beast of a man vill tear you to pieces in front of us all!'

'Conor would never do that,' Diana managed to say, her voice choked with jealousy. Lifting her head, she added with pride, 'He's an old friend of mine.'

Talia laughed under her breath. 'He's an even older friend of mine, dahlink, and I tell you—zat man has a temper!' She placed a red-taloned hand on Diana's arm, drawling, 'Oh...he is passionate!'

Diana's mouth shook with impotent rage as Talia swayed off, magnificent in her black witch's costume, black hair flowing down her slinky back, a silver spiked crown on her head.

The heat was burning her bare shoulders: jealousy was burning her insides. She wondered in one brief moment of hysteria if spontaneous combustion were on the cards.

Looking bitterly at Conor, her heart skidded to a standstill as she saw Talia Hite was now standing beside him, red talons currently sliding over Conor's broad shoulder, firm and powerful beneath his white shirt.

Jealousy scorched her. Shaking, she watched Conor bend his dark head to Talia's and whisper something in her ear. Talia threw back her glossy head and laughed.

Diana couldn't stand it any longer. She got up, white with pain, and walked back to her trailer.

He was going to take her advice. The truth hit her as she closed the trailer door and stood there, breathing harshly. He was going to take Talia and drop her. Maybe he had already taken her...maybe he had been telling the truth last night...maybe he had made love to Talia last night.

Why should I care? she almost screamed aloud, but the tears stung her eyes like hot needles and only her pride stopped her crumbling in front of the make-up and wardrobe people who watched her.

That evening, Geoff caught her as she arrived back from the shoot, hot and dusty and in need of a shower as always.

'Hi!' He looked very cool in fresh jeans and a white shirt. 'Had a good day in the fields, darling?'

She was beginning to feel as though Geoff might be her only friend, and was genuinely glad to see him. 'Oh, Geoff!' she said huskily, putting a hand on his arm. 'It's wonderful to see you! I——' To her everlasting chagrin, tears burst into her eyes and she had to look away, a hand to her mouth. 'Oh!'

'Diana!' He was instantly concerned, taking her arm and leading her to one side of the hall, holding her upper arms gently and saying, 'What on earth is the matter? Diana, please...tell me!'

She shook her head, struggling not to make a complete fool of herself by crying. 'I—I just had a really bad day.'

'Slade?' Geoff asked deeply, studying her closely.

Diana hesitated, then nodded, saying hoarsely, 'He was absolutely bloody to me. I—I forgot my lines, fluffed cues all over the place...' She gave a husky laugh. 'I even broke one of the props!'

'Oh, you poor thing!' Geoff put his arms around her, drawing her against his chest, and Diana went gratefully, her face cool in the shade of the marble hallway as he stroked her hair, saying, 'Which prop did you break?'

She laughed huskily against his chest. 'The glass casket!'

'Oh, dear!' Geoff stroked her hair. 'And they had that specially made...'

'Conor almost breathed fire!' Diana told him, trying hard not to cry at the memory of his tight-lipped, terrifying patience. 'If he'd shouted at me, I'd have been able to stand it, but he didn't. He just fumed silently and sat there hating me for the rest of the afternoon.'

'Poor darling! Never mind—it's only seven o'clock, and we're having dinner tonight—remember?'

'Oh, yes...' Diana said huskily, feeling rescued from an evening of heartbreaking solitude and self-hatred. 'Oh...that'll be wonderful! I can't think of anything I'd like to do more than have dinner with you tonight, Geoff! It's just——'

'How touching!' Conor bit out tightly behind them, and Diana turned with a gasp, breaking out of Geoff's arms, her face flushed and her eyes wild with shock. 'On-set romances always flare up between the most unlikely candidates,' Conor said, 'but they rarely last, and rarely end happily. I hope you both know what you're doing!'

'You've got a nerve!' Diana said under her breath, hating him. 'When I think of——'

'Hastings,' Conor broke in, blue eyes flashing dismissively past Diana's angry face, 'you left the set at lunchtime. Why?'

'I——' Geoff cleared his throat, pale and anxious. 'Well, I had to study the script alterations, and I thought it best if I——'

'You need my permission before leaving set,' Conor said bitingly, 'as you very well know. See me in the library at seven-fifteen sharp tonight.' He strode away, his face hard and angry.

Diana stared after him furiously. What priceless remarks about on-set romances! He had the nerve of the devil, he really did! Trying to seduce both his leading ladies with every trick in the book, and then he delivers a speech like that on an innocent friendship! She could have screamed!

'What an absolute bastard!' Geoff said when Conor was out of earshot. 'Did you hear what he said?'

'I heard!' Diana said under her breath, heart thudding with anger.

'He told me himself to have those script alterations ready for tomorrow morning.'

Diana turned to look at him, brows lifting. 'And he expected you to do them tonight?'

Geoff grimaced. 'I wanted to take you out...'

'Well, I guess you're just going to have to face the music,' Diana said tightly, 'and, from the look on his face, it's not going to be Beethoven's *Ode to Joy*!'

He studied her carefully. 'We're still having dinner, though?'

'If you can make it, yes!'

'Great! I've booked a table at the best restaurant in town. It's called Roi de Soleil.'

Diana stiffened. 'Roi de Soleil...' It was the restaurant Conor had taken her to when they had first arrived here. The memories it would invoke would be unbearable.

'You'll love it!' Geoff kissed her impulsively on the nose, smiling as he stepped back. 'I'll go to the library now—be early. Impress him with my professionalism!' He laughed, calling, 'Meet you down here at eight!'

Diana went to her room, trying and failing to imagine how it would feel to be at Roi de Soleil tonight with Geoff instead of Conor. It only made her see how completely she loved Conor.

Suddenly, the differences between Conor and Geoff glared at her and she winced, unable to face them right now. There were too many unfaceable realities. She couldn't cope with any more.

Stripping her clothes off, she walked, naked, into the bathroom. It was a cool sanctuary, and Diana stepped into the beautiful rose enamel bath, switched on the shower and gasped as the hot needles pummelled her tense shoulders.

Water was cascading over her head, flattening her long hair to her scalp and right down her slender back as she pushed rich conditioner through it, enjoying the sensual feel of the glutinous wax as it slid over and coated each hair.

Soaping her body, she felt her pulses race. She couldn't help closing her eyes as she slid soapy hands over her breasts, thinking of Conor, of those long, strong fingers and the feel of them on her breasts, her belly, her thighs...

Heat was invading her body, arousal springing from just the memory of Conor: just the thought of him. God! He didn't even have to be physically present to make her blood throb and her thighs quiver with desire.

She hated him! Oh, but if only he were here! If only there were some way to take what she wanted so badly, to take his love, his physical love, to give herself up to the desire coursing through her veins and to just make love to him as though they were both going to be executed at dawn...

Tears stung her eyes and she whispered fiercely, 'I *am* like her!' She looked through the steamy, hot, damp bathroom at her flushed face in the mirror, saw her passion-blazing blue eyes, the soapy nudity of her body, and whispered, 'Allannah Sullivan!'

She forced herself to look into her face, her mother's face; her eyes, her mother's eyes; and suddenly she heard her voice whisper angrily, 'So what?'

Diana ran a hand through her wax-slicked hair. The water was pounding on the enamel bath, splashing angry droplets on to her thighs. 'She was my mother,' Diana murmured, turning her body to the water and slowly, sensually washing the soap from her breasts, her nipples erect as she went on, 'Why shouldn't I be like her? It's only natural...'

Her hands ran over her belly, and her pulse-rate was throbbing higher as she thought of Conor, thought of his hands on her belly, thought of his children inside her. And what children they would be! Black-haired gypsies with passionate blue eyes and quick, clever minds...

Fantasy took over, and she closed her eyes, swaying as the water pounded over her body, her mind filled with vivid images of Conor as her lover, her husband, the father of her children...

But dreams never come true, she remembered with sudden pain, and felt tears burn her lashes as she opened her eyes, and was just a woman alone in her bathroom, listening to the hail of water all around her.

Frustration burned in her like bitter gall. She turned, eaten up with the fire, and put her head under the water, raking her hands with angry gasps of frustration through her hair. She raked them through again and again, almost crying, and suddenly she realised her hair had been clean for ages, and that it was squeaking, clean and shiny and sodden with water.

She stepped out of the shower, wrapped a pale blue fluffy bath-towel around herself, opened her bedroom door and walked across the floor.

'Oh!' She froze, staring in shock at the sexy, dynamic, passionate man lying on her bed, and her first instinct was to slide into his arms, make love to him, run her fingers through his hair and whisper her love as he ran his strong hands all over her. The blood was pulsating like wildfire in her veins. She wanted him...she loved him...he was everything to her, everything, everything, everything...

'Hi,' Conor said softly, his body lazily predatory as he lay, hands behind his head, one long leg bent with the kind of masculine arrogance that made Diana's eyes shoot across his body with ill-concealed desire.

'Hi,' she answered stiffly, clutching her towel to her breasts. 'What are you doing in here?'

'What do you think?'' he asked coolly, watching her through heavy lids.

'Trying to annoy me?' she suggested angrily, hating herself and him for the arousal she was fighting so hard to conceal.

'Now, would I do that, darling?' he drawled, eyes mocking.

Her mouth tightened. 'I thought you were seeing Geoff.'

'Geoff...' He frowned, then bit his lip. 'Oh, yes—you mean Hastings? Don't worry. I've booted him around a bit. Just to teach him a lesson. I doubt he'll try to skive off again. Certainly not with me around.'

'He wasn't skiving off!' Diana said at once. 'He was——'

'Taking you out to dinner?' Conor said softly, and the edge of steel in his voice made her shiver. 'Yes, he told me all about that. That's why I've——'

'Geoff told you?' She was amazed he could be so indiscreet. Hadn't she told him that she'd once been involved with Conor?

'Yes, he's a malleable boy, isn't he?' Conor drawled with satisfaction.

'He's not a boy!' she said angrily, her face flushing.

'Oh?' Conor's eyes narrowed. 'You have proof of that, do you?'

Her flush deepened and she said angrily, 'Of course I haven't! What do you take me for?'

'I don't know that I take you for anything,' he said under his breath, uncoiling, his blue eyes very intent and his mouth very hard as he got slowly off the bed and to his feet. 'In fact, I'd be very interested to hear just what exactly you think you're doing with Hastings.'

'I'm having dinner with him,' she said, more nervous now that he was standing. 'Is that a crime?'

'It is if it leads to bed,' he said through his teeth.

There was a tense silence. Their eyes met and warred. Diana was the first to look away, overwhelmingly conscious of her nudity beneath the towel.

'I'm not obliged by law to answer your unspeakably insulting questions,' she said huskily, 'but, since I'm almost naked and you're a ruthless bastard, I feel I would be well-advised to do so. Therefore——' she looked up, her blue eyes angry and hurt '—mind your own damned business!'

'All right, Diana!' he said softly, watching her with narrowed eyes. 'Put it like this. Either you answer my question, or I'll come over there and take that towel away from your particularly delectable body.'

She caught her breath at his insolence, staring. 'You...you wouldn't!'

'Come on, Diana! We both know I'd like nothing better.'

She hated him, but she forced herself to say thickly, 'What was the question?'

'Do you intend to go to bed with Hastings?'

Her mouth trembled and she said angrily, 'You know perfectly well I don't!'

'Good,' he said slowly, nodding. 'But if he tries to seduce you—what then?'

Diana hesitated. The last thing she wanted was for Geoff Hastings or any other man to try and seduce her. Geoff was very sweet, very kind, very sensitive, and she liked him enormously. But Conor made her heart race. Conor filled her bloodstream. Conor felt like the other half of her soul, and although she hated her helplessness in loving him she could not deny that she did.

But she couldn't tell Conor that! She might just as well throw away all pride and fling herself into his arms telling him she was desperately in love with him. Just the thought was humiliating...

'You're taking too long,' Conor said tightly. 'Answer immediately or say goodbye to that towel!'

Bitterness flashed in her eyes and she said hoarsely, 'Go to hell!'

He laughed and walked towards her, eyes furious.

'Don't you come near me!' Diana said shakily, backing, clutching her towel. 'And don't try to bully me! I can't defend myself against you!'

'Don't try to appeal to my sense of fair play,' he said tightly, standing in front of her threateningly. 'I haven't got one where you're concerned!'

'Develop one!' she said huskily, and her back hit the wall. She looked up at him with startled eyes and heard her voice whisper pleadingly, 'Don't come any closer, Conor! And don't...don't do anything! Not while I'm like this. I'm defenceless and you know it!'

'Yes...!' he said softly, his hard thighs pressing against hers as she caught her breath and her hands went to his broad shoulders. 'It's when you're defenceless that I want you most.'

'Don't, Conor!' she burst out hotly as his hands went to the knot of her towel.

He stopped, long fingers tucked into the front of her towel, just about to whip it away at the slightest move. He looked at her and his blue eyes made her legs buckle at the knees.

'Shall I?' he asked softly, tugging at the towel.

'No!' she returned, shaking, her face scarlet. 'No!'

'Give me one good reason why I shouldn't!'

'Because...' She moistened her lips.

'Can't think of one?' He tugged at the towel and it began to slip.

'No!' Her voice was hoarse. 'Please...!'

Conor smiled and put a hand against her thudding heart, murmuring, 'You want me to, Diana. You just haven't the courage to admit it!'

'Please don't...!' she whispered through parched lips, her whole body throbbing. 'Please!'

'All right,' he said, toying with the knotted towel at her breasts while she trembled helplessly, staring at him, 'I'll tell you what I'll do. We'll make a deal. A little wager, between ourselves.' The blue eyes flicked up to meet hers and he was unsmiling as he said softly, 'Soul to soul. Lover to lover. Man to wife. A deal you must keep to: regardless of later circumstances.'

She held her breath, nodding. 'All right...what—what is it?'

His face was flint-like as he said deeply, 'The deal, my love, is this: if you cancel your dinner date with Geoff Hastings, I will leave you alone—forever.'

CHAPTER EIGHT

DIANA stared, thunderstruck, and felt the colour drain from her face. Of all things, she hadn't expected this. Conor's face was so deadly serious, his blue eyes so grave, and his mouth so hard that she could hardly take in what he had said. She couldn't imagine being near Conor without being involved with him. Even though it hurt to know he didn't love her or care for her, she still welcomed his touch with that sweet, tortuous passion. Her body betrayed her every time, and as she stared at Conor now she realised she had been hoping that her physical attraction for him would make him love her ...

'I mean, it'll be over,' Conor said thickly, unsmiling. 'Finished. Kaput. You'll never see me again except on a professional basis. I'll tear it all up, turn to Talia, and chalk you up to experience.'

She swallowed, pain ripping through her. 'You ... you mean if I cancel my dinner date with Geoff, you'll never try to kiss me again? Or—or touch me? Make love to me?'

'That's exactly what I mean,' he said deeply, mouth hard.

She had been hoping all right! Bitterness flooded through her as she saw her hopes dashed to smithereens on the floor. She had been hoping that he would grow to love her, that if she held him off for long enough the scales would tip in her favour. What a fool! What a stupid little fool!

'That's what you want—isn't it, Diana?' Conor asked under his breath, his face stony. 'For me to leave you alone? Well—here it is. I'm offering it to you on a silver platter! Take it!'

It hurt to speak. It hurt to look at him. Suddenly, it hurt to be alive.

'Of course it's what I want!' she said hoarsely. 'I—I just hesitate because I feel sure there's a flip-side to the deal!'

He nodded slowly, looking directly into her eyes. 'Oh, there is. You can go out with Geoff Hastings for dinner tonight, and I'd be none the wiser.'

'Yes, of course!' she bit out, swallowing hard, struggling not to break down in front of him.

'But——' Conor held up one long finger, dark brows rising, '—if you do go out with him tonight, you break our deal. And then I must have recompense.'

She moistened her lips. 'Re—recompense?'

'A penalty,' he said softly, watching her. 'And the penalty is—you go to bed with me.'

Her heart stopped beating. She should have seen it coming. For a long moment she couldn't speak, and, as she stared at his tough ruthless face, at the scar on his cheek and the passion in his eyes, she felt such a conflict of love and hate that she almost flung her arms around him and half killed him with a kiss.

'Let me get this straight,' she forced herself to say eventually. 'If I cancel with Geoff tonight, you'll leave me alone. But if I don't cancel: you'll claim my body as forfeit?'

'You've got it,' he said under his breath.

Diana's mouth trembled. 'Well, you can just stuff your crooked deal right up your nose!'

He laughed, blue eyes mocking. 'Worthy sentiments! But, I'm afraid, the deal has already been struck. There's no going back now, Diana. You're in this up to your neck, and, believe me, I shall claim my penalty prize with pleasure if you rat on the deal!' He turned swiftly on his heel, striding away from her with a smile of hard triumph.

'What do you mean—the deal has already been struck?' she called after him furiously. 'I didn't agree to it! Not once did I——'

He turned at the connecting door and drawled, 'You did agree to it, Diana. You asked me not to take the towel off, and I didn't. Fair is fair!' He opened the door.

'But I didn't know it would be this kind of a deal!'

'It's perfectly simple, Diana,' he explained, smiling lazily. 'You have a choice. You can cancel your date,

and get rid of me forever. Or you can go out with
Hastings and pay the penalty.'

'But that's not fair!' she said, fuming.

'Life isn't fair!' was his reply, eyes wicked as he went
through into his bedroom.

The door closed behind him, and Diana stood alone
in her bedroom wondering if she had gone mad. When
had she made the deal? How? He had offered her the
deal and she had agreed to listen to it ... but that was
because he'd backed her up against the wall and was
about to remove her towel, leaving her stark naked and
defenceless!

Frustration welled up in her. Now what was she supposed to do? Cancel Geoff? How could she do that when
he'd got his ears boxed on her behalf? Conor had said
he'd kicked Geoff around for taking the afternoon off—
it would be monstrous of her to then cancel the date.

But if she went and Conor found out ...

She exhaled shakily, moving to the dressing-table, eyes
flicking to the clock nervously. It was seven-forty-five.
She had precisely fifteen minutes to make up her mind.

Geoff was in the hallway, spruce and bright-eyed in a
lightweight grey suit, his pale blue-striped shirt open at
the throat. He smiled when he saw her.

'Bang on time!' He watched her walk down the stairs
in her bright blue, romantic off-the-shoulder dress, long
blonde hair floating like silk as she moved. 'And don't
you look ravishing?'

'Thank you, Geoff,' she said huskily, kissing his cheek
briefly, 'and you look charming, too.' Anxiously, she
darted glances around in case Conor was in the vicinity.

'Everyone seems to have had the same idea as us tonight,' Geoff told her, taking her arm. 'Conor and Talia
have just gone out to dinner and——'

'What?' Diana stopped short, staring at him, her skin
bleached white and her eyes enormous.

'Yes, they left a few minutes ago,' Geoff said lightly,
gesturing to the drive outside. 'See? No Slade-mobile.'

Diana stared out at the dusty bleached drive with the
tall thin trees framed against a golden twilight sky.

Conor's rented blue Citroën was conspicuous by its absence.

'They went to dinner?' she asked in a tense, brittle voice. 'Together? You're sure?'

'Of course,' Geoff said, surprised by her question. 'In fact, they're going to the same restaurant as us—Roi de Soleil.'

'What?' This time, Diana took a step back, appalled, then said in a rush, 'We can't go! You'll have to cancel! We mustn't go to that restaurant, Geoff, or——'

'But why?' he asked, frowning, touching her hand. 'It's such a good restaurant. It's even in the Michelin guide, and——'

'Please!' she said through dry lips, heart hammering. 'I can't go there with you, Geoff. I can't explain why. Just believe me, please—either we go to another restaurant or I'll have to——'

'Are you still involved with him?' Geoff asked at once, staring.

'No, of course not!' she said huskily, racking her brains, then saying, 'It's—it's just that we don't get on. And if I go to the same restaurant it'll ruin my evening.'

'Well, that's OK,' Geoff said, smiling. 'Easily solved. I'll cancel our reservations at Roi de Soleil and book somewhere else.'

Diana breathed easier, swallowing hard, her throat dry. 'Yes... that would be wonderful.'

'OK,' he said gently, 'wait here...' And he turned, disappearing down the corridor.

Diana breathed a sigh of near-despair. Geoff was so kind and sweet. How could she let him down? Of course, she was frightened Conor would find out, but in the circumstances how could he? He was out with Talia.

Her mouth tightened. How dared he tell her to cancel her date with Geoff when he was going out with Talia? His arrogance defied description.

Geoff's footsteps echoed in the marble hall. 'All done!' he said cheerfully. 'I looked in the Michelin guide and found a great restaurant about thirty kilometres away. We can get there for nine o'clock if we leave now.'

They drove along intensely Bonapartian roads lined with trees. Gold light dappled the bonnet. Geoff played a Prince tape and talked about his life, his ambition to become a director one day.

St Raphael was a small, pretty town of bleached buildings and leafy trees. The restaurant was an ivy-covered *auberge*, and as they entered they were greeted warmly by the *maitre d'*, and shown to their table.

Diana chose *crevettes* followed by *truite armandine*. Geoff chose *moules marinières* followed by *cailles*. They talked lazily as they ate and the wine was poured.

'Slade was an absolute bastard tonight,' Geoff remarked as he cut a quail on his plate. 'It was like being reprimanded by my headmaster!'

'He can be very cutting,' Diana agreed, eyes angry.

'To say the least! But then, he's ex-SAS, isn't he?'

'It helps him direct battle scenes,' Diana said, burning inside with jealousy as she pictured Conor at this moment making love to Talia. 'This is his kind of film.'

'Yes.' Geoff nodded. 'But it's not mine.'

'And what is?' she asked, desperate to stop thinking about Conor.

'*Brideshead*,' Geoff smiled. '*Room With a View...*'

'Really!' Her brows lifted with a smile. 'Straw hats and parasols?'

'Absolutely. And isn't that the kind of picture you'd rather be doing, Diana? You're so perfect for it...long floaty dresses and croquet on the lawn.' He laughed. 'You're so terribly British, innocent and sweet!'

Diana looked at him and thought of Conor Slade, of a blood-red sky above the dark Celtic mountains of Connemara.

'*Encore du vin, mademoiselle?*' said the *maitre d'*.

Diana looked up, eyes alive with emotion, and across the restaurant she saw Conor Slade standing at the entrance, magnificent in black evening suit, scar on his warrior cheek as he looked across at her with a hard smile of triumph.

'Oh!' Diana caught her breath sharply, reeling under the impact of that hard stare. Her eyes flashed to Talia

Hite, slinking in beside him, slithering a black mink from her bare shoulders, diamonds flashing at throat and ears.

'*Mademoiselle...?*' enquired the *maître d'*, concerned.

'Diana?' Geoff leant forwards. 'Is everything all right?'

Conor was walking towards her, Talia at his side, and she was suddenly on her feet, shaking, her face death-white as she broke out hoarsely, 'Excuse me, please!'

She was shaking as she walked to the ladies' powder-room, barely able to reach it and shut the door before she even asked herself that vital question: How did he know we were here?

Diana stared at the pink carpeting, walked slowly to the pale pink and gold brocade chair in front of the mirror, and sank down on it, staring at herself in the mirror.

How had he known?

Was Geoff in on it? No! She couldn't believe that of him. He was a decent young man, kind and sensitive. He wouldn't have connived with Conor Slade to get her here under false pretences so Conor could claim his— she swallowed hard, staring at herself—his forfeit!

Would Conor do it? Her heart thudded too fast. Would he? She could hardly believe he would feel justified in doing so—not as he was with Talia Hite. After all—the way he had made that 'deal' with her had not only been underhand, but loaded with the implication that he personally was staying in to brood alone all night.

The door swung open. Diana looked up with a shock as Talia slinked in in a clinging black strappy number edged with diamanté, her heavily lidded eyes drooping with superiority as she studied Diana.

'Dahlink!' she purred, slinking into the seat next to Diana. 'Repairing your *maquillage*? How vonderful! I vill join you!'

Diana fumbled with her handbag, taking out lipstick and a comb, struggling to appear confident beneath that patronising gaze.

'I lof your hair,' Talia drawled. 'Is it quite natural?'

'No,' Diana said huskily, tensing as she applied pale pink lipstick, 'I have it coloured. I'm naturally a brunette.'

'Really?' purred Talia, applying jungle-red lipstick. 'Vell, votever possessed you to change it?' She ran a red-taloned hand through her glossy black hair. 'Gentlemen may prefer blondes, but who vonts a gentleman?'

Diana put her lipstick and comb away, flushing.

'Personally,' Talia drawled, spraying on Dior's Poison to wrists, throat, cleavage, and ankles, 'I like a reeee-al man!' Green eyes flashed to Diana with cat-like malice. 'Like Conor Slade, for instance. And let me tell you, dahlink, he is no gentleman!'

Diana looked at her through dark lashes and felt such intense jealousy that her blue eyes flashed out silent hostility to the other woman.

'But, then,' purred Talia, satisfied, 'I think perhaps you already know that. Hmm?'

Diana said nothing, burning inside and refusing to be baited.

Talia got to her feet in one slink, smoothed her long fingers over her dress, and moved to the door, drawling, 'See you in ze morning, dahlink! I must go and please my director...!'

For a long time after she had left, Diana sat alone, surrounded by the scent of Poison, seething inside with more emotion than she had ever felt in her life.

But she had her pride. And she had to pull herself together; to go out with her head held high and make them both see that she wasn't going to be defeated just like that. And, even though she felt brutalised and bitter inside, she managed to draw a deep breath, open the door, and go back out for battle.

Conor watched her as she walked to her table. Her heart thudded with awareness and she did not look at him, but her body moved for him, and she felt those blue eyes burn obsessively over her curves as she swayed in her blue off-the-shoulder dress, slender and sensual and seductive.

Deliberately, she bent to Geoff as she reached him and whispered, 'Look who's here!' in his ear before sliding into her seat, heart thudding as she concentrated on not looking at Conor.

'Good heavens!' Geoff exclaimed, turning back to her. 'He told me he was going to——'

'The Roi de Soleil,' Diana said tightly, trembling as she sipped her wine. 'Quite. It seems he changed his mind.'

'How incredible!' he said, and frowned. 'Do you think we should go over and speak to them?'

'No,' Diana said thickly, spilling a little wine on the tablecloth. 'No, I think they prefer to be left alone...'

Somehow, she managed not to meet Conor's burning gaze for the next twenty minutes. By the time coffee had arrived, she was a nervous wreck, her whole body jumping with awareness of him, desperately trying not to notice that he occasionally touched Talia's hand and murmured things she would not have been able to tolerate overhearing as he made love to her with his eyes over the table.

'More coffee?' Geoff asked.

'No, thanks,' she said huskily. 'I'm rather tired, to be honest...'

He nodded. 'I'll get the bill.'

Diana flicked a sharp look at Conor and recoiled from what she saw. He was kissing Talia's wrist! I hope he gets a mouthful of Poison! she thought savagely, and got to her feet, blue eyes bright with pain.

As she left the restaurant with Geoff, she did not even glance at Conor. Outside, it was dark, and the stars gleamed as the moon waned. Geoff opened the car door for her. She slid inside, crippled by pain.

Eleanor had been right. Conor wanted nothing but sex. Look at him with that siren, that vamp, that black-haired witch. What did he want from Talia if not sex?

They sped across the countryside. Diana stared into the darkness and struggled not to think of Conor with Talia, Conor kissing Talia, Conor telling Talia he loved her...

They turned into the gates of the château, drove up the drive towards that dusty, bleached triptych gleaming under the moon, and as the car slowed, the pain over Conor's betrayal grew deeper.

'A nightcap in the drawing-room?' Geoff suggested as they walked into the marble hallway.

'It's been a wonderful evening,' Diana said huskily. 'But I'm exhausted, Geoff. I must go to bed.'

'Do you mind if I walk you to your door?' he asked with a smile.

She didn't have the heart to say no, so she just smiled, and a second later they were walking up the stairs, along the corridor, and Diana's mind was filled with Conor, filled with him as though she *was* him, as though life without him was nothing more than a death sentence...

'Well,' she said with a pained smile as they reached her bedroom door, 'here it is.'

'And here's my goodnight kiss...' Geoff said softly.

A second later, his hands were on her waist and his blond head bending to kiss her. Diana closed her eyes, submitted to his kiss, and felt nothing. Nothing at all. Just a pleasant, warm kiss with a friend. Her soul cried out for Conor, like a woman wailing for her demon lover.

'Oh God, Diana!' a thickly aroused voice suddenly said, and her eyes flashed open in shock just as Geoff caught her in a fierce grip, opened the bedroom door and started manhandling her into the room like a maniac.

'Just a minute...!' Diana gasped out.

His mouth silenced her, and Diana squirmed, fighting him as they went staggering and tumbling backwards into the bedroom together.

'Get off me!' Diana choked out, but his tongue was drilling into her mouth, she couldn't get away from those hot, squeezing hands, and the whole thing was a nightmare as she found herself being pushed towards the bed.

'Yes!' Geoff was blind with passion as he kissed and squeezed. 'Yes...!'

'No!' Diana turned into a whirlwind of slapping and scratching to escape him, crying out as she fought.

He stumbled back, a hand at his face. 'Ow!'

There was an appalled silence. Blood marked his cheek. Diana was breathing hard, fear in her eyes.

'I'm sorry,' she said shakily. 'But you shouldn't have done that.'

He stared, his hand still at his cheek. 'You scratched me!'

Diana tried to stay calm. 'Geoff, I'm sorry! But I didn't want you to do that, and I didn't encourage you to——'

'Yes, you did!' he said angrily. 'You've been leading me on for days!'

She gasped incredulously. 'I have not!'

'You have and you know it!' he said furiously. 'By the time I took you out tonight, I thought it was understood that I'd——'

'Geoff, for heavens' sake——'

'Well, why do you think I took you to that place tonight?' he exploded, blue eyes flashing. 'The bill was a week's wages for me! You don't think I spend that kind of money on——'

'But I thought you wanted to be friends with me!' she whispered, her face white as the awful truth sank in.

'At that kind of price?' he said unpleasantly. 'Forget it!'

Horrified, she just stared at him, trembling, her face white.

'And don't think you can rat on me about this,' Geoff said suddenly, his eyes rather worried, 'because I'll deny it! I'll just deny the whole thing and——'

'Don't worry!' she said thickly, contempt in her eyes as she flicked her gaze away from him. 'I shan't be broadcasting the incident on national TV!'

His mouth tightened. He raked a hand through his hair, saying angrily, 'How can I believe you? You'll tell Slade, I know you will!'

'I won't tell anyone!' she bit out, looking back at him. 'Now please, just go. We'll forget it ever happened!'

Geoff hesitated, then turned on his heel and slammed out of the bedroom.

Diana sank on to the bed, her mind reeling. So Geoff had thought she was leading him on. She could scarcely believe it. How had she led him on? How on earth had she given the impression that she wanted him to make love to her?

By accepting that date with him? she thought suddenly, her eyes pained. By kissing him today in the hall? By turning to him this afternoon and flinging myself in his arms because Conor was crucifying me on set and off?

A deep sigh wrenched her. Yes, she could see Geoff's point. But not where that disastrous seduction attempt was concerned. Surely he had been able to see that she didn't *enjoy* his kisses? That she didn't *want* him to kiss her? That she was struggling and filled with distaste by his kiss?

She grimaced, compassion for poor Geoff filling her. How awful that she should have felt repelled by his kiss. It had been so horrible, though. That drilling tongue...

Diana shuddered.

Best to just forget it, she thought, and got up, undressing slowly, selecting an ivory silk nightdress and négligé and putting them on her naked body.

Standing in front of the mirror by moonlight for a moment, she studied herself and felt acutely alone. So beautiful, so much a movie star, and so horribly alone.

Tears sprang to her eyes. She walked across to her bed and lay down on it, staring into her darkened bedroom and thinking of Conor, thinking of the past, of how deeply in love with him she had always been and how deeply in love she still was.

Love wasn't anything like the great poets would have her believe. No fairy-tale romance or sugar and spice. Her love for Conor was nothing but madness...

Suddenly she thought of Talia Hite seducing Conor, and she burned with jealous rage. I bet Talia Hite doesn't think twice about making love to him like a wildcat!

'The little witch!' Diana said fiercely to herself, sitting up on the bed in the dark and torturing herself with images of Talia and Conor. 'How dare she...with my husband?'

But he wasn't her husband any more...

The tears burned her eyes, and she heard so much silence in her bedroom at that moment that she felt even more acutely alone. Her eyes moved to the connecting door.

Without thinking, she got up and walked slowly to the door. She turned the handle. It was unlocked. Sighing deeply, she walked into Conor's bedroom.

It was pitch-black inside. Diana felt for the light, flicked it on. Such a very masculine room...the dark wood four-poster bed, the ties hanging over the wardrobe door, the newspaper on the bedside table—*Le Monde*—and the black jacket flung carelessly over the chair.

Walking into the room, she found herself standing by the chair, and knew before she reached it that she wanted to pick up his jacket and smell his scent clinging to the expensive black material.

It was a relief to snatch it up, hug it to herself and move dreamily to the bed. She sank down on it in her ivory silk négligé, blonde hair spilling over her shoulders as she closed her eyes, breathed in Conor's scent from the jacket and crumbled inside with love.

When she opened her eyes, Conor was standing in the doorway.

'Oh——!' She leapt up, flushing and flustered. 'I—I didn't mean to——'

'Yes, you did,' he said deeply, closing the door behind him.

'I—I was just feeling lonely,' she stammered, putting the jacket down, 'I—I came in to——'

'To see me.' He was walking towards her, his eyes intent. 'Admit it, Diana. You've got to——'

'I did not come to see you!' she denied huskily, trying to back off and realising she was trapped by the bed. 'I was lonely, I tell you, and I wanted to——'

'Darling,' he murmured, hands sliding on to her waist, blue eyes burning on her cleavage, visible where the silk nightdress ended, 'I think I've waited for this for so long, that I might just——'

'What do you mean?' she burst out, shaking, staring at his hard face. 'I didn't come here for that!'

'Yes, you did,' he said huskily, and bent his head to kiss her mouth. 'I knew as soon as I saw you at the restaurant that——'

'How did you know I was there?' she asked without thinking. 'It was a ten-to-one shot, a chance in a million that you'd walk in and——'

'No, it wasn't,' he drawled, mouth sardonic, 'because I lent Hastings my Michelin guide.'

'He used your Michelin guide...?'

'Yes, and I'd circled that restaurant in red and written, "Perfect for seduction evenings" beside it!'

Her lips parted. 'What? My God, of all the devious, low-down——'

'You didn't have to go,' he drawled, eyes mocking. 'I wasn't sure that you would, not until the moment I drew up outside and saw Hastings's car parked there. But, even then, I couldn't be certain it was you he was with.'

'You set me up...' she whispered, heart thudding with sudden understanding.

'You set yourself up,' he said softly. 'Don't kid yourself!'

Her face flamed. 'I did no such thing! I just——'

'Accepted the date?'

'Yes!'

He laughed under his breath and drawled, 'Ever heard the old saying, "You pays your money and you takes your choice"?'

'What choice?' she breathed, heart stopping dead.

One long finger ran over her mouth. 'To make love to me. What else?'

Diana stared for a long tense moment. He couldn't mean it! Go through with that stupid deal he'd made earlier? After what she'd seen tonight?

'You're mad!' she said at last, her breathing erratic. 'You really think that ridiculous wager has some validity?'

'Of course,' he said, frowning, 'and so do you. That's why you went out with Hastings and why you waited for me, here, in my bed.'

'What?'

'Well, that is what you've done, Diana,' he drawled, blue eyes mocking as a sardonic smile touched his hard mouth. 'I mean—you can't get round the facts, and those are the facts!'

'But——!' She could scarcely speak, fear choking her throat as she struggled to breathe, her heart thundering against her breastbone.

'The wager was clear-cut, my love!' Conor drawled, studying her mouth. 'If you went out with Hastings, you made love with me. If you didn't, I left you alone forever.'

'But I didn't know!' she said huskily. 'I thought you wouldn't find out if I——'

'That's irrelevant, Diana,' he said, dark brows rising. 'I said you had to keep your side of the bargain, regardless of the circumstances.'

Terror engulfed her and she said fiercely, 'But that's not fair! I didn't think you'd seriously——'

'Regardless of the circumstances!' he said again, mouth hard. 'Facts, Diana. Facts. You went out with Hastings; you waited in my bed for me. There's really nothing more to be said!' His eyes flashed a warning as his dark head lowered for the first kiss.

'No!' Panic made her push hard at his broad shoulders, eyes flashing. 'After you've been with Talia Hite? What's the matter with you? Do you think I'm stupid?'

He frowned. 'You must know Talia is only——'

'Talia is your mistress!' Diana said fiercely, blue eyes hating him with sudden passion. 'I've seen you together!'

'Only the camera never lies, Diana!' he said flatly. 'And what you——'

'Which is more than can be said for you!'

'I don't deal in lies!' he said, eyes hard. 'Talia Hite is not my mistress and never has been!'

'Oh!' Jealous fury blazed in her eyes and she said angrily, 'How can you live with yourself? You're beneath contempt! Not only can I see what's going on between you with my own eyes, and not only did you once tell me yourself that you and Talia had had an affair, but Talia herself virtually spelled it out to me in neon letters tonight!' She was shaking, blood pulsating through her veins as she at last unleashed all the jealousy, possessiveness and hurt he had caused her.

'Talia told you?' Conor flashed back. 'What the hell are you talking about?'

'In the ladies' powder-room!' she snapped, hating him. 'Where else would a woman like Talia unsheath her claws? Certainly not in front of her man, that's for sure! She's too smart for that!'

Conor laughed, but his eyes were angry. 'And what exactly did Talia say?'

'I can't remember!' she said fiercely. 'I was too busy fighting off the fumes of Poison!'

He laughed again, eyes dropping to her mouth. 'You little bitch!'

'Me? Well, I like that!'

The blue eyes flicked wickedly to hers. 'Go on,' he drawled, 'I love to see you shake with jealousy!'

She did. Right in front of him. Her mouth tight, her eyes blazing with passionate emotion, and her full mouth quivering as she controlled the urge to kill him.

'You're jealous,' he said under his breath. 'Admit it!'

'Go to hell, you ruthless bastard!' she cried in sheer despair.

'Admit it!' he demanded thickly. 'Why shouldn't you? I'm prepared to admit I'm jealous of that little bastard Hastings! My God, I've been itching to punch him on the nose for days, and if you tell me anything I don't want to hear about him, I'll have my excuse and do it!'

Diana was staring at him, blue eyes alarmed.

Conor's shrewd mind worked like lightning. 'He did something, didn't he?' he bit out suddenly, eyes fierce as he gripped her waist. 'What did he do? Tell me!'

'No—nothing...!' she said shakily, knocked off-balance by his violent jealousy.

'Liar!' He was suddenly darkly flushed, his eyes glittering. 'He kissed you! Yes—I can see it in your face. But there was more, wasn't there? My God...I'll kill him! I'll kill the little——'

'He didn't do a thing!' she said hoarsely. 'I swear it!'

'It's written all over your face, Diana!' he spat, nostrils flaring, and suddenly released her, running both hands through his thick black hair, pacing up and down in front of her like an angry lion. 'What was it? How far did it go? Who ended it? Who——?' He broke off, staring at her, eyes raging as he asked hoarsely, 'He didn't——?'

'No!' she whispered hotly, shaking her blonde head. 'No...nothing like that.'

Conor stared, breathing harshly. 'Then what? What did he do, Diana?' His eyes raged over her face. 'Tell me or I'll——'

'He kissed me,' she blurted out in a husky rush, face flaming. 'We fell back into the room, can't remember how, doesn't matter...'

'He was in your bedroom?' he bit out between his teeth.

She flinched. 'It—it wasn't deliberate! He walked me to the door, and when he started to kiss me—I don't know, it just happened!'

'What just happened?' he asked, eyes dangerous.

She moistened her lips. 'He...he caught me because I nearly fell. Then his hands were all over me and I——'

'What?' He leapt back to her, gripping her shoulders in iron hands. 'Tell me he didn't go too far!' he said hoarsely. 'Tell me or I'll go completely berserk!'

'No,' she said at once, trembling, 'he just kissed me and—and touched me.'

'Where did he touch you?'

'Conor, for God's sake!'

'No!' he bit out, mouth shaking. 'Diana, for God's sake! You know I'm going up in flames right now, so unless you want me to burn this whole damned château to the ground you'd better do something fast to stop me exploding like a fireball!'

She looked at him and said quickly, 'He touched my breasts through my clothes. That's all. Nothing else.'

Conor watched her, breathing hard, staring at her with those glittering, passionate eyes.

'I swear it, Conor,' she said, and her heart thudded as she tentatively reached out a hand to run it over his broad shoulder, moving up to his throat to feel his pulse throbbing wildly as she went on, 'Nothing else happened.'

Conor expelled his breath in a harsh, tense sigh. 'Well,' he said flatly, watching her, 'that's very lucky for Hastings. Now I'll only break his knees instead of his neck.'

'Don't be so ridiculous!' she murmured, a smile touching her mouth as she finally admitted to herself and to him her delight in his jealousy and the thrill it gave her to see that there was a lot of passionate emotion in what Conor felt for her. 'He didn't know...'

'Oh, didn't he?' Conor said flatly. 'Well, he must be blind as well as stupid! I thought I'd made it obvious to all and sundry that you were mine!'

'I don't think so, Conor,' she said angrily, stiffening. 'You've spent more time with Talia than you have with me!'

He gave a tight smile. 'Don't bring Talia back into this. I've told you. She is not and never has been my mistress!'

'And I've told you,' she said angrily, 'I don't believe you!'

His eyes flashed. 'And I don't care, Diana, what you believe, because I made a deal with you and now I intend to claim the forfeit!'

CHAPTER NINE

THE silence was so fraught with tension that it was almost as though live currents ran between them, frazzling both of them, making it impossible to do anything other than stand face to face, body to body, both eaten up with passion and a need that was suddenly clamouring to be satisfied. Hunger, Diana thought as her heartbeat thudded like an African tribal drum and she felt the ancient vibrations in her blood, her skin, her soul.

'You think I'll let you take me?' she said softly, watching Conor through her lashes. 'After everything that's happened between us?'

'That's precisely why you'll let me take you,' he said under his breath, 'because you and I are both going to go insane unless I get you on that bed and we earth this madness together!'

Her thighs were trembling, excitement coiling like a tight spring in her belly. 'Madness is a very apt description. This has no basis in reality!'

'It doesn't need one,' he said thickly. 'It's got nothing to do with buildings and banks and jobs. It's a much deeper reality than that. It's made of fire and blood and passion, and we really ought to be in Connemara, Diana!' His eyes blazed on her mouth. 'We really ought to be on those mountains again beneath that——'

'Blood-red sky!' she whispered, and Conor inhaled sharply, staring at her for a second in electric silence. Then he took a step forwards and the madness exploded between them.

They were clinging together and his hard hot mouth was ravaging hers as they fell back on to the bed, landing in a tangle of passion, each making harsh sounds of excitement as Conor stripped the jacket from his back and flung it to the floor.

He was tugging her négligé down, his hands shaking on her bare breasts, nipples so hard that she moaned aloud with fierce excitement as he touched them, and

then her hands were at his shirt, unbuttoning it, gasping
as she pushed it aside to bare his tanned, hair-roughened
chest.

'Oh, God!' Conor was saying thickly as Diana blindly
pushed his shirt off, threw it to the floor, and Conor's
hot mouth was on her breast, sucking hungrily, then a
second later Diana lifted herself with a moan, her mouth
sliding over his bare chest as his heart thundered against
his ribcage.

They were blind in their passion, like desperate
drowning lovers as they twisted together, united totally
for the first time in their desire as Conor pulled Diana's
nightdress down over her hips, breathing harshly as he
saw her, saw her slim thighs and her naked body already
sheened in sweat.

'Conor...!' she was whispering fiercely, watching in
a frenzy as he pushed the clothes from his own body,
pushed them down to expose his own magnificent, masculine, hair-roughened nakedness.

He came back to her, his mouth clinging to hers as
he slid between her thighs, and they were clawing at each
other as his manhood throbbed against her, and a second
later, with a series of harsh gasps of desire, he pen-
etrated her.

'Oh, God...!' Diana moaned hoarsely, twisting beneath him, impaled by him, staring into his hard, sweat-
dampened face, and then a second later he drove into
her with a series of brilliant thrusts and she felt the
pleasure so deep that it was as though her womb were
coiling up, tighter and tighter, and, as her hands raked
his back and his mouth ravaged hers in a violent kiss,
she felt that womb tighten into the brink of madness and
a second later she was crying out in agonising pleasure,
flipping up and down like a rag-doll as the hot wet
spasms dragged her down into the blackest, hottest hell
she had ever known.

'I love you...' Conor was biting out thickly. 'Oh,
God...!' and his whole body jerked into her as he too
was racked by the spasms and flung screaming into hell,
his heart banging as though in cardiac arrest as he

writhed on top of her, and Diana was blindly gasping
out words of love on his damp shoulder, her eyes rolling
into the back of her head as she came to a standstill of
exhausted love.

For a long time they lay in silence, both breathing
raggedly, their heartbeats as loud and violently pulsing
as the blood that throbbed through their drained bodies,
and the feeling of hot, sticky love that united them made
Diana feel—for the first time in six years—alive. Fully
alive, truly alive—a woman; a creature of flesh and
blood, given life in order to crash through the womb
screaming, and suffer tragedy, disaster, love, passion,
heartache, pain, joy, despair and pleasure before leaving
at the end of that lighted passage that was life, pre-
sumably screaming with as much shocked incredulity as
she had entered it.

I love him, she thought as her hand stroked his damp
hair, and a smile touched her mouth as she knew suddenly that she could take it. Believing that love was *nice*,
she thought, was what was keeping her from loving
Conor. And this, although delicious and irresistible and
violently pleasurable, was hardly what any sensible
person would call nice.

They lay like that for a long time in silence, each
thinking their own thoughts.

Conor raised his head suddenly to look at her. Diana
met his eyes with a ruined wisdom that matched his, and
he smiled but said nothing. There was a long silence as
they studied each other, Diana motionless, Conor
motionless.

Then he stirred inside her.

She felt the throb deep in her centre, and her heartbeat
leapt into life again as she heard Conor's breathing
quicken. He moved inside her, and she started to kiss
him, opening her mouth to his as their bodies began to
slide against each other, and a moment later they were
making love in an intensely passionate silence, his hands
gripping her as he drove on and on and Diana drove
against him, her body on fire. He took her to a higher,
darker abyss in that telepathic silence, and as he flung

her into hell he drove against her, biting out hoarsely, 'Yes...! Yes...!' before his body rocketed against her in blind release and he fell, shaking and crying out too, their bodies pulsating with hot drumbeats of pleasure.

They lay together for a long time in silence. The scent of fresh sweat in Diana's eyes, hair and nostrils was so wonderful that she kept breathing it in deliberately, aware that her scent was mingling with his and that was as it should be.

In the darkness, they both heard the clock chime the hour softly from the mantelpiece.

Conor lifted his dark head and his eyes were glittering as he murmured, 'How do you feel?'

'Ruined,' she said softly, meeting his gaze.

He smiled. 'You look it. And I love to see you like this. I love it...' His mouth kissed hers tenderly as he said deeply, 'Welcome home!'

Diana clung to him, tears burning her eyes, and whispered, 'I love you, Conor!'

'Darling!' He held her very close, arms tight, so tight around her that she knew he loved her as desperately as she loved him, and for a long, long time they held each other in silence, their minds brushing one another and acknowledging the joy, the relief, the deep consuming unity of their souls.

After a while Conor raised his head and said deeply, 'It's late. We should sleep.'

'Yes,' she agreed huskily, stroking his damp hair.

He separated himself from her and she felt the sense of loss deep in her soul, but, as he dragged the covers over them and pulled her into his arms, she was complete again, her arms going around him when she laid her head on his chest and fell asleep listening to that heartbeat, to the blood pulsing slower and slower around his body as the waves of peace lulled them both into sleep.

The telephone shrilled into the pitch-black bedroom at four-thirty a.m. It had a dream-like quality to its sound, as though it had no business to ring because it had no place in their world, the world of lovers, the world of Slade and Sullivan.

Diana answered it without thinking.

'Yes?' she murmured into the mouthpiece, eyes dreamily closed.

There was a crackle in her ear. Then a voice said, 'Mr Slade?'

Diana said automatically, 'Hang on, he's just——' Recoiling, she broke off, staring at the telephone as though it were alive.

Conor was watching her in the darkness, a wry smile on his hard mouth as he held out one hand for the receiver.

'Oh, no,' Diana whispered, wide awake now, 'it was your phone...'

'And you answered it,' he said softly, dark brows lifting with amusement.

Diana groaned inaudibly, handed him the phone and hid her face in his chest as his arm came around her and held her while he propped one elbow to the side and put the phone to his mouth.

'Yes...' His voice was deep and husky, and Diana toyed with his chest as she listened to his heartbeat before his voice said, 'Right. I'll be down shortly and so will Miss Sullivan.'

He replaced the receiver.

'I could just die!' Diana said into his throat.

'I shouldn't bother,' he drawled. 'If last night didn't kill you, nothing ever will.'

'But they'll all know...'

'Who cares?' he said simply, and stroked her hair.

Diana hesitated, anxious about her reputation for a second, then the warmth of him claimed her and she relaxed against his chest, saying, 'Yes. Who cares? They all seem suddenly irrelevant...'

'Other people are always irrelevant when you have something like this,' he said deeply.

'There are two worlds, aren't there?' she said huskily. 'One full of things like money and buildings and jobs and problems, and the other——'

'Full of heather,' he said softly, stroking her hair, 'and the scent of lovers.'

She smiled, studying his chest. 'Oh. You know it too.'

He laughed and kissed her. 'I'm afraid we're going to have to go out into the other world in a moment. Think you can cope? I mean—we haven't had a chance to talk yet.'

'Can we talk tonight?'

'Not until very late,' he murmured. 'Don't forget it's Talia's party tonight.'

'Oh, you're kidding!' Diana groaned. 'Whose idea was that?'

'Talia's. She badgered Georgina into it. At any rate—we'll have to attend.'

'You're right,' she agreed softly, 'but we can slip away early—can't we?'

'Just touch my hand and say: "Connermara, darling"', he said deeply, 'And I'll know what you mean.' He kissed her mouth, pushed back the bed-clothes, and stood up, his body magnificent as he turned and said softly, 'See you on set, Diana Sullivan...'

Diana stretched lazily, flaunting her nude body in cat-like delight, and Conor laughed under his breath, blowing her a kiss before going into his bedroom and closing the door.

For a long time she just lay in bed, smiling benignly and thinking of him. Then she forced herself to get up and take a shower, feeling regret as she washed the scent of him from her body.

In a dream of love, she dressed in an ivory lace dress, brushed her long hair and knew it was dark, although it looked blonde, then went downstairs feeling she could live with anything, survive anything, now that Conor was hers again.

As she passed the library on her way to the dining-room, she heard Georgina's voice.

'Darling, you must tell her.'

Diana stopped, frowning in the cool marble corridor, dawn light filtering through from the windows.

'How can I possibly tell her at this stage?' Conor said deeply. 'It's gone too far! She genuinely believes I'm in love with her and about to——'

'Tell her you don't love her,' Georgina drawled wryly. 'Perfectly simple matter.'

Diana had frozen, her face draining of all colour. The pain was suddenly flooding her so fast that she almost couldn't stand, couldn't move, and could not have walked away from those unacceptable voices if her life had depended on it.

'But you know she's unstable!' Conor was saying. 'And she's just had such a terrible shock! How can I possibly break it to her gently? She might go completely to pieces!'

Sweat broke out on Diana's pale forehead.

'She's very highly strung, I agree,' Georgina said worriedly, 'but that's why I asked you to take her on in the first place.'

Diana swayed.

'And I should never have listened to you, Georgina!' Conor said deeply. 'I should have had more sense. Now I'm in it up to my neck, and the worst part is, I haven't——'

'I know, I know,' Georgina said quickly. 'It's not your fault. It's all in her own head.'

'Precisely,' Conor said. 'And that's why I suggest we call in some kind of psychoanalyst. Someone she can talk to on a daily basis, while we carry on filming. He could sit with her in her trailer for an hour a day. It could be arranged, couldn't it?'

'Do you know,' Georgina said slowly, 'that might be the perfect solution?'

'I hope so,' Conor drawled, 'I can't stand playing father-figure to her any more! Not while she's whirling it all up into a grand passion that doesn't exist!'

Somehow, Diana found the strength to move, her stomach forcing her to as it churned with nausea. She was running, white-faced and sweat-dampened, down the corridor towards one of the bathrooms, running into it and leaning over the rose-patterned enamel just before she retched violently.

Gasping for breath, she lifted her head, then retched again, shuddering, tears in her eyes.

How could he have done it ... how? Pain racked her so violently that she thought she might retch again, but as her hands gripped the sink with white-knuckled fingers she felt it recede, and as the nausea left so that pain grew.

He told me he loved me first! she thought with fierce pride: I would never have confessed it like that if he hadn't!

She had thought she could cope with love last night when he'd made love to her, but now she knew she had deceived herself in a moment of over-emotional foolishness, and she couldn't believe any woman could be so stupid, so gullible, so sentimental ...

Tears burst from her eyes and she covered her face with her hands, thinking: Conor thinks I'm unstable! He's been playing me along in order to keep my performance up to scratch for the film!

She felt ashamed and full of self-hatred, then she thought: No! Why should I feel like this when he's the one who's been playing games with me? All I did was fall for them!

Anger surged through her, saving her from despair, and she felt it take the sting out of the pain, just a little, just enough to give her the courage to face the wreckage of her love and of her life.

It so happened that today they were filming the battle scene.

Diana arrived on location at eleven o'clock. The sky was filled with cannon smoke, extras lay dying on the battlefield in bloodstained uniforms, and the battle raged in the furthest field among gunfire.

'Company C—attack!' Conor hurled orders through a walkie-talkie. 'Close-up on the King, camera six!'

Diana stood watching him, her red eyes hidden by dark glasses. He didn't even notice her arrival. Crushed beyond belief by his betrayal, she turned and walked to her trailer.

'Dahlink!' Talia was sitting outside her own trailer on a body-rest. 'Vy do you alvays look so desolate in ze mornings? Is it a man?'

Diana stopped walking, and just looked at her, boiling with rage.

'Don't stare at me like that!' Talia laughed. 'Anyvone vould zink you vere mad!'

The humiliation of it! Diana strode to her trailer, tears stinging her eyes, and had to go through the process of make-up and costume without being able to confide her turbulent emotions to anyone.

When she was called, she went outside to the battle-field to find Conor waiting for her.

'Darling!' He raced across to her, his eyes alive with excitement as cannon smoke filled the air. 'You look absolutely ravishing! Give me a kiss!'

She recoiled, horrified. 'Don't touch me!'

His head jerked back, eyes widening in shock.

'Just tell me where I'm to ride into shot!' Diana said tightly.

He stared at her, then said deeply, 'Diana . . . what the hell is wrong?'

'Nothing!' Her mouth shook. 'Just give me my directions and——'

'Don't be bloody ridiculous!' he bit out thickly, gripping her wrist. 'I can see perfectly well that you're upset about something! Now in God's name—what is it?'

'Nothing!' she choked out fiercely. 'Now let go of my arm, Conor, or I'll kick you where you most deserve it!'

His jaw dropped open. 'What?'

'You heard!' she said bitterly. 'Now show me my positions and——'

'I damned well won't!' he bit out. 'Not until you tell me what——'

'Sir, we're running close!' the assistant director shouted. 'She's got to ride in three minutes or we've blown it!'

'All right!' Conor said bitingly, then turned back to Diana. 'I can't believe you're doing this!' he said under his breath. 'After last night——'

'Let me go, you bastard!' she hissed. 'And don't throw last night in my face or I'll——'

'Sir!' The assistant was frantic. 'Two minutes, twenty seconds!'

'Hell!' Conor raked a hand through his black hair, then leapt into action, hustling Diana over to the unicorn. 'Get on it!' he ordered and then hoisted her up with his strong hands. 'Ride straight through the soldiers to the witch's chariot...'

Diana listened bitterely to his instructions, hating him.

'One minute!' shouted the assistant director.

'...kill the witch,' Conor was saying, 'take her wand, ride up the hill towards the King...'

'Forty-five seconds!'

Conor looked into Diana's eyes. 'Diana, for God's sake!' he said thickly. 'Tell me what's happened or I'll never forgive you! I can't believe you're doing this!'

'I'm here to act!' Diana said hoarsely. 'Not have sordid affairs with my director!'

He sucked in his breath, eyes hellish. 'After last night, you little bitch, how can you say——'

'After last night,' she said bitterly, 'you have no right to expect anything from me but contempt!'

'Contempt!' he said hoarsely. 'Why you——'

'Twenty seconds!'

'How can you feel nothing but contempt?' Conor was shaking with rage. 'How can you justify——?'

'Sir!' The assistant was leaping about with his stop-watch. 'Talia's chariot is rolling into the——'

'All right, damn it!' Conor shouted, and slapped the unicorn on the rump. 'Ride!'

Diana rode into battle, blonde hair flying behind her as the hot tears rolled angrily down her face, and blood-stained soldiers parted for her as she rode down on Talia, blinded by jealousy and hatred as she killed her, took her wand and rode up through the cheering crowd to the King.

Two hours later, her work was done, she had hung up her costume, removed her make-up, and it was time to go home and let the stand-ins finish the battle scene for her.

Diana ran for the minibus, a straw hat on her head and dark glasses shielding her tear-stained eyes. Conor didn't see her leave—he was too busy talking to Talia.

The château was her sanctuary for the rest of the afternoon. At six-thirty, she saw from her balcony the trucks rolling back along the dusty road, and she knew Conor was back.

She dressed in a long blue statin strapless dress with a thick diamond choker around her throat. Then, before Conor could get upstairs and demand an explanation, she hurried downstairs and out into the grounds of the château.

The warm breezes calmed her, the scent of hot grass, clusters of roses and honeysuckle and bougainvillaea making her feel as though she had a friend in Mother Nature.

She waited out there until eight o'clock, avoiding Conor until she heard music from the ballroom and knew the party had started. Then she made her way, sick with nerves, towards it.

The first thing she saw was Conor dancing with Talia.

Gasping aloud in pain, Diana pushed her way across the crowded ballroom and stumbled to the terrace, sick inside, the heat and noise of the party like a nightmare.

The cool evening breeze on the terrace calmed her. Hot tears stung her eyes as she stood there in the open french doors, swaying with pain, and looked at the dying golden sun, the colour of the death mask of Agamemnon.

Suddenly, she saw two people in evening dress across the lawn. They were lovers in love, kissing, their bodies clinging together as Diana watched in an agony of pain.

When they slid apart and walked towards the french doors, Diana's eyes widened in a hammerblow of shock.

It was Eleanor! Eleanor and James Carthax, and as Diana stared at them, she felt her world tilt on its axis, because she had never before seen her guardian with a man—not like this.

'Diana!' Eleanor saw her from a few feet away and stopped dead for a second, clutching James's hand.

James bent his austere silver head to Eleanor and said something. Eleanor shook her head violently, but James insisted, and slowly, slowly, she let go of his hand and moved towards Diana.

For a second, the two women looked each other in the face, the darkness around them, the only light that which spilled from the ballroom doors.

'Diana,' Eleanor said stiltedly, 'I feel I must attempt some kind of explanation.'

'I would be very grateful,' Diana said, watching her steadily.

'I——' Eleanor broke off before she'd even started, then clumsily touched Diana's arm, saying, 'I don't know how I can ever——'

Diana recoiled instinctively from Eleanor's touch.

'Oh, dear God!' Eleanor withdrew her hand at once from Diana's arm and turned to James. 'I can't even begin to do this!'

James urged her, turning her back to Diana, 'Eleanor, you must!'

'She won't even let me touch her!' Eleanor hissed, red lips tight. 'What's the point...?'

'It wasn't deliberate,' Diana said at once, 'I just did it without thinking. I——' Anger flashed in her blue eyes momentarily, then she said under her breath, 'You must understand, Eleanor. You've never touched me before. It felt so...so unnatural and I——'

'Don't say any more,' Eleanor cut in, shaking her head, 'I understand better than you think. I only wish I could find the words to explain...to apologise. It—it was all so long ago, and so complicated, so stupid...'

Diana moved towards her urgently. 'My mother...?'

'Yes,' Eleanor said, watching her face. 'You see—oh, God, I find it so difficult to talk about, even now!'

Diana said at once, 'Please— Eleanor, I have to know.'

Eleanor looked at her, tightened her lips, looking old again suddenly in the light spilling from the ballroom as she forced herself to say thickly, 'My sister—your mother—stole my fiancé.'

'My mother,' Diana echoed, 'stole your fiancé from you?'

Eleanor nodded stiffly. 'He was your father, Diana. My fiancé; Charles Fitzpatrick; your father. They are one and the same man. He was engaged to me before he met Allannah.'

'Oh, no!' Diana said huskily, staring, and felt the final piece of the jigsaw puzzle hurtling towards her.

Eleanor closed her eyes, mouth tight. 'I must go on, though how I shall find the strength...'

'Remember what I told you,' James said, austere but supportive at her side. 'It's the only way to put it all behind you once and for all.'

Eleanor looked at him, then nodded, and her voice roughened as she said, 'I'll say it quickly, then.' She steeled herself, then said in a rush, 'They met at my engagement party. I was eighteen, and Allannah twenty-four. She'd just been widowed. Her first husband was very old, very rich——' She broke off, staring at Diana. 'Are you following this?'

'Yes,' she said quickly, though she was struggling to grasp it all.

Eleanor took a deep breath. 'He died two years after they were married, but Allannah hated him. My parents had married her off in order to seal a business deal, and she never forgave them because I think her husband was vicious to her.'

'My father was her second husband?' Diana said, leaning weakly on the balustrade wall of the terrace as the sun shone gold on her white face.

'Yes.' Eleanor nodded stiffly. 'I was my parents' favourite, though. And I was allowed to choose my husband.'

Diana looked at her and said huskily, 'Poor Allannah...'

Eleanor's eyes filled with blue pain. 'I saw her looking at Charles across the ballroom as though thunderstruck, and Charles looking back at her with that same wild passionate need in his eyes.'

Diana said, 'It was love at first sight?'

'Yes,' Eleanor said flatly, 'and I couldn't begin to try and forgive until it happened to me.' Her hand groped for James, and he moved quickly to her side, his face serious as he put an arm around her slim shoulders. 'You see, Diana—I just didn't believe them. They told me they tried so hard to stop it happening, but I didn't believe them.'

'And because you didn't believe them,' Diana said slowly, 'you thought it had been deliberate.'

'Yes! They kept telling me they were helpless in its grip! But how could I believe them? I thought Charles loved me! I—I thought I loved Charles. But we were friends, really: not lovers.' A sigh broke her red lips. 'I thought I understood love...'

'We all feel that way at eighteen,' James said deeply, squeezing her shoulders.

'And I more than ever,' said Eleanor 'because my sister had always been disapproved of in the family. When she eloped to Ireland with Charles Fitzpatrick——'

'My mother eloped...' Diana stared '...to Ireland!'

'Yes,' Eleanor admitted. 'That's why I almost lost my mind when you did the same thing with Conor Slade. Can you imagine how I felt when I got that telephone call?'

'Yes!' Diana said, wide-eyed, as everything finally fell into place.

'I was so tortured by bitterness!' Eleanor said, eyes blazing. 'I never recovered from that first elopement. I was stuck there. A jilted bride for eternity! And I just got more and twisted up inside! It was inevitable that I should try to ruin your life just as my sister had ruined mine. But the awful truth is that I ruined my own life...'

'No!' James said deeply, turning her to face him as the tears blurred Eleanor's eyes. 'The wheel has come full circle now, Eleanor! You're a woman in love and the wounds are going to heal!'

'Oh, James,' Eleanor said thickly, putting her head on his shoulder, 'if only that were true! I sometimes think I shall never forget!'

Diana at once stepped forwards, putting her hands on her guardian's shoulders and saying huskily, 'You're my half-mother. You were always there for me, even though I knew you hated me. How can I not try to understand why you did it? How can I not try to forgive?'

'I've ruined your life!'

Diana smiled. 'I'm only twenty-four—I have time on my side.'

'But I've stolen so much of your time!'

'No,' Diana said, eyes pained, 'just a little here and there. And without you I wouldn't be here, would I? I would have been put in a home for orphans, and...' her mouth trembled in a smile '...that really would have been sad!'

Eleanor looked at her, her face suddenly bitter again. 'I don't deserve such forgiveness!'

'Yes, you do!' Diana said, feeling the circle finally reach completion. 'Just as my mother and father deserve it from you. We all deserve forgiveness, Eleanor. After all—we're only human.'

'A touching speech,' Conor's dark voice said thickly from the open doorway. 'A pity you don't always have the strength to live up to it!'

Diana whirled, catching her breath, and anger flooded through her as she met that hellish blue gaze and hated him for listening to the long-awaited reconciliation between her and Eleanor.

'Conor,' Eleanor's voice said stiffly, 'I don't know how much you heard, but I don't doubt you wanted to hear it. Or——' her mouth tightened '—or that you needed to. I wronged you, too, and——'

'Please.' Conor shook his dark head, walking towards them as red light began to streak the sky. 'I understood a long time ago.'

'Did you...?' Eleanor was incredulous.

'Of course,' he said deeply, and as he reached her he raised his brows and said coolly, 'I didn't know what had happened, but I knew you must have been badly hurt to react like that.'

Diana stared at him. How could a man so brutal and selfish be so perceptive?

'You're all so kind,' Eleanor said stiffly, 'and I've been so cruel!'

'You've just been unhappy,' Conor said, 'And now— it's time for you to be happy, instead. James... I believe this is your cue.'

'Thanks, Slade,' James said gruffly. 'We won't forget this.'

Conor smiled, and then his smile faded, blue eyes flicking to look at Diana, and suddenly the atmosphere frazzled with electricity as Diana met that hellish gaze and felt her body wrench in response.

Eleanor and James exchanged glances.

'We'll go and get some of Georgina's lovely champagne,' James said carefully. 'Coming, darling?'

They moved away into the ballroom, leaving Conor and Diana facing each other on that terrace, the sky behind them a glorious mass of blood-red and orange.

CHAPTER TEN

'WELL?' Conor asked deeply, blue eyes penetrating hers.

Diana drew a shaky breath. 'You shouldn't have listened to any of that, Conor. It was—very underhand of you.'

'Come on, Diana,' he said flatly, 'I've been a victim of her past, too.'

'Have you, Conor?' Diana asked huskily, looking at him as tears shimmered in her eyes.

'Of course!' he said harshly, moving towards her. 'You know damned well I got hurt!' He gripped her upper arms, blue eyes passionate. 'And I'm hurt still, Diana! I can't understand how—how we got from last night...to this.' His gaze rested on her eyes, saw the bitterness there and he said thickly, 'Can't you tell me about it? Tell me what's happened to make you ... hate me?'

'Nothing's happened, Conor!' she said on a hoarse sob. 'I just grew up, that's all!'

'Grew up?' he repeated dully, staring. 'It doesn't make sense ... nothing that's happened today makes sense. I left you this morning after the most passionate night of my life, and——'

'Passionate?' Her eyes were filled with bitter tears.

'Yes, damn you! Passionate! I just keep reliving that moment in my mind. When you looked at me and said it ... and I knew you hadn't forgotten it either. I knew you'd carried that sky in your heart just as I'd carried it in mine ...'

'Yes!' Diana looked at him, her mouth trembling. 'But how could you have used it like that, flung it at me so cheaply, just to get me into bed and——?'

'What?' His eyes blazed like blue fire. 'Are you crazy? How can you possibly believe the rubbish you're talking? Diana——' He gripped her tighter, his voice hoarse as he said, 'You felt it, too. I know you did. I saw it in your eyes. That moment of dawning, that moment of absolute recognition. My God, I was so moved by it ...'

'Moved straight into bed with me!'

'No!' He breathed harshly, and the sky was quite red, turning his tanned skin to beaten, burnished, bloody gold. 'No, it wasn't like that. It was deeper, way deeper than any physical expression of love could ever hope to go.'

She looked into his passionate eyes and felt uncertain. 'I ... I notice you still tried to express it as fully as possible in——'

'Of course I did!' he said huskily. 'And so did you!'

Her face flamed and she quickly looked down, murmuring, 'Conor, I was just a fool ... a silly romantic fool who got what was coming to her. I believed in you ...' she raised her eyes, tears falling over her lashes now '... I believed in you and paid the price!'

'What price?' he demanded. 'A night like that? It was everything I've ever believed love could be. It was every love-poem I've ever read, every epic love-story I've ever seen on film, every great love-affair from history...'

'Oh, you're so damned clever!' Diana whispered, aching inside, desperate to believe him, desperate to throw her arms around him and cling to him against that sunset.

'Darling,' he said rawly, 'last night you made me feel like Mark Antony...like Heathcliff...like——'

'Stop it!' she whispered, closing her eyes against the bitter tears that threatened to fall.

'I can't,' he said thickly, gripping her even tighter, 'not now. Not after last night. I was prepared to let you go yesterday. I was beginning to believe you really meant it. It really was over. You really were going to go with that pest Hastings!'

'Oh, don't say any more!' she whispered, her head shaking to dispel the terrible confusion and uncertainty his powerful words invoked.

'That's why I made that deal with you,' he said under his breath, eyes intent. 'I had to. I had to throw the biggest spanner in the works that I could find. Anything—anything to stop you going into another man's arms, and I knew I had to throw it fast.'

'No...' she whispered. 'You just wanted to——'

'So I made that deal,' he said thickly. 'I put everything on your number, Diana, and hoped the wheel would spin in my favour. And it did. You went...'

'I didn't know you'd been so devious!' she said hoarsely, feeling such a fool for having been tricked.

'I had to be! I knew you'd never go to Roi de Soleil with him, and so I gave Hastings my Michelin guide and said perhaps he should try somewhere else because I was taking Talia to Roi de Soleil.'

Diana looked at him uncertainly. 'But you were with Talia!'

He gave a grim laugh. 'Darling, I have a lot of courage, but even I balked at the thought of walking into that restaurant alone to see you with another man! But I had to go there. I had to catch you out and claim the forfeit, and——'

'Don't say any more!' Diana said brokenly, almost choking on her unshed tears. 'I can't bear to hear these lies, these——'

'And I knew, then, when I saw you in the restaurant, that you wanted me. I knew you loved me. I knew it, was sure of it, yet so unsure, Diana...so unsure deep inside. But when I opened my bedroom door and found you there, holding my jacket to your cheek, with your eyes closed and such love in your face...'

'I didn't mean to do it!' she said huskily, shaking her head. 'It was an impulse...a stupid impulse...'

'I knew you loved me,' he said deeply, eyes burning into her soul. 'But I wasn't sure when and how you had loved me. I just stood there in the doorway, looking at you, and thinking: Has this only just begun? Or has it been there...' his voice deepened '...buried inside her for six long years, buried under the blonde hair and the fear and the layer upon layer of guilt?'

Diana stared into his eyes in silence. The warm breeze lifted strands of her hair, the diamond choker at her throat glittering, ablaze with red light from the dying sun.

'You went white when you saw me,' Conor told her deeply, 'just as you've gone white now. I remember you were shaking...and I remember you were embarrassed. As though I'd stepped suddenly into your fantasy, and seen the deepest part of your mind.'

She said huskily, 'I felt such a fool...I felt angry and stupid and hurt!'

'Why?' he asked urgently. 'For showing your love? For the first time in six years? For admitting it to yourself and, by chance, to me?'

'More so for showing it to you!'

'But that wasn't the moment that united us, Diana,' he said deeply, and raised one dark brow. 'Was it?'

She met his dark, serious gaze, his face aglow with red light, and suddenly knew there was no point in lying any more, in pretending, in trying to save her stupid, foolish pride. Regardless of what she had heard this morning, she *did* love Conor. She loved him body and soul, and now her pride felt stripped away, leaving her with nothing but her feelings, however bruised and battered. He might see her as unstable and unlovable, but what did that matter when she felt this much?

'No,' she saw rawly, lifting her chin with the dignity of love. 'No, it wasn't the moment that united us, Conor. I remember the moment very well. It was when you spoke of Connemara.' Her voice shook. 'And it was like the wind suddenly pushing through my hair! I could smell the heather and feel the grass beneath my bare feet, and we both stepped forwards at the same moment and fell on to the bed in the most...oh, God, Conor...the most passionate tangle of love!' Her eyes blazed. 'But you shouldn't have done it, Conor! You shouldn't have used Connemara to get me into bed! It was cheap and contemptible and...and it feels as though you've desecrated it! Now I'll always think of Connemara and feel used! Abused! Defiled!'

'How can you say that?' he demanded hoarsely, eyes burning with hurt rage. 'How can you, after——?'

'Because I overheard what you said to Georgina this morning about me!' she burst out suddenly, unable to control herself any longer.

There was a long stunned silence. Conor was holding her upper arms in a tight grip, but his face was shocked, and as he stared at her she saw the disbelief in his eyes and felt again that prickle of uncertainty.

'I heard you, Conor!' she said rawly, as though to convince herself more than him. 'I walked past the library before breakfast. I heard what you said...I heard!'

'The library...' he was staring '...Georgina...'

Her eyes hated him. 'Do you want me to repeat the whole conversation word for word?'

He studied her for a long moment, thinking hard, and suddenly his eyes flashed with realisation. 'You don't mean—you can't possibly mean——?'

'Every last word, Conor!' she said hoarsely, and gave a raw sob, the tears suddenly winning as her control slipped away and, to her intense humiliation, she broke down in tears in front of him, a hand going to her mouth as she whispered hoarsely, 'Oh, God! Please don't let me cry...please!'

'But, my God...' Conor put a hand under her chin, pushing it up '...Diana, I wasn't talking about you in the library with Georgina! I was talking about Talia!'

Diana looked at him in misery through her tears and whispered, 'No more lies...I couldn't take it...'

'Listen to me!' he said under his breath, and turned his dark head, looking over his shoulder quickly before guiding her as she cried weakly, a hand at her mouth, to the white steps that led down to the bleached lawns. 'Diana. You must listen to me——'

'There's just no point,' she said brokenly, but allowed him to lead her down the steps and on to the lawn, her high heels sinking into it. She kicked them off, standing barefoot, suddenly even smaller as he towered over her tiny, curvaceous figure.

'All right,' he murmured, nodding. 'I can understand why you feel like that. But let me tell you a little bit about Talia. OK?'

Diana closed her eyes against the tears, drawing a shaky breath.

'Talia Hite is not her real name,' Conor said deeply, taking her hands in his and watching her intently. 'She was born Talma Hudge in a little mining town in Kent.'

'What?' Diana's eyes flashed open.

'Yes,' Conor said with a wry smile, 'she's really just an ordinary girl who wanted to be extraordinary. And she did it, to a certain extent. I mean—she's beautiful, famous, successful, rich; everything she set out to be.'

'Talma Hudge...' Diana repeated, staring.

'But she's not real,' Conor told her. 'Everything about her is false. The accent, the manner, the phoney past: everything.'

'My God...' Diana could scarcely believe it. 'But she's fooled the whole world!'

He nodded. 'Yes. Including everyone who knew her way back when she was Talma Hudge.'

'But...' Diana was perplexed '...surely someone recognised her?'

'Cosmetic surgery,' he said deeply.

'Oh!'

'Not that much,' he amended, frowning, 'but, with green contact-lenses, a perfect Russian accent, publicity men pushing her phoney aristocratic past and the muscle of the film-world backing her to the hilt, she made it without a hitch. Nobody even suspected, and if they did they couldn't prove it.'

'It's incredible,' Diana said huskily. 'I believed it completely.' Her mind suddenly clicked into action as she remembered the exact nature of the conversation she'd overheard this morning, and she suddenly heard herself say, 'No wonder she's unstable.'

'I think she might be on the brink of a complete breakdown,' Conor said quietly.

'Oh, no...!'

'Her father died last month,' Conor said. 'She read about it quite by chance in Dover on her way over here. She hadn't seen or spoken to him for ten years.'

Diana's eyes closed. 'Poor Talia...'

'Yes. And you can see why both Georgina and I are frantic about her. Georgina asked me to step in when she arrived and give her the absolute maximum of my attention without turning it into a romantic illusion. Well, I did my best, but of course she's swinging wildly at the moment, and she just is not stable enough to handle any kind of attention from me.'

'Especially as you were once involved with her,' Diana said.

'We weren't lovers, though, Diana,' he said deeply. 'You must believe that. We really were just good friends. But not that good. Never that good. For instance—I didn't know she wasn't Talia Hite the Russian actress until she arrived here to start filming.'

'You're kidding!'

'No,' he shook his dark head, 'she just blurted it all out to me within half an hour of arriving. It was incredible. Like a haemorrhage of some kind. All those startling truths spilling out left and right and centre, and I kept staring at her and thinking: Oh, my God, she's just about to crack into a million pieces.'

Diana winced and said urgently, 'But she shouldn't be acting in this condition! You should get her to a psychiatrist right——'

'I am. I've arranged for a specialist to fly in from Zurich tomorrow morning.'

She breathed a little easier. 'Does Talia know?'

'That's the tricky part,' he drawled, mouth crooking wryly. 'But if she refuses to see him I'll make it clear that she'll be fired. Of course, I wouldn't dream of firing her at this point in her life, but I've got to do something.'

'Are you sure she'll be all right?'

'Well, I think it's best if she continues to have a structure to her day, if she finishes this film with psychiatric help and then flies to Switzerland for full rest and treatment. After all—she does have a great deal of pride, and she seems to have kept the problem contained on set. Also, her role isn't actually that big. We'll only need her for a couple of weeks at the studio.'

Diana nodded, sighing as she looked away and thought of Talia, remembered her spite and deliberately provocative remarks, and saw them now in such a different light that she could hardly believe she'd been so blind and unfeeling. And selfish, she realised, because where Talia was concerned she had only ever stiffened with stupid jealousy and pride, and that had prevented her from seeing that anything might be wrong with Talia.

'So,' Conor said thickly, his hands suddenly reaching for her, sliding on to her waist as he drew her towards him, 'does that make any difference to your feelings towards me?'

Diana looked up at him and whispered, 'Oh Conor...I'm so sorry!'

'Darling!' He pulled her against his broad shoulder, his strong arms tightening around her. 'I never doubted you. Not really. There were moments when I was so afraid you'd stopped loving me that I even began to believe you'd *never* loved me! That I'd imagined the whole thing...created a great sprawling love-affair in my own head out of sheer loneliness...'

'Don't!' she said urgently, her arms around him, her face pressed against his hard chest. 'I've been so lonely, too! So desperately alone and afraid! Sometimes I couldn't bear to open my eyes in the morning and face another day...'

'Another day without love!' he said hoarsely, his mouth against her hair. 'Oh, God, yes! It was a life sentence...an empty pillow beside me forever...and no one else could fill that space, no one else's eyes could watch me live, no one else's mouth could fit so well against mine...'

'And no one else's body,' she said huskily, looking up into his eyes, 'could ever fit so perfectly with mine!'

'Oh, my love, my love!' he whispered fiercely, his mouth burning down on hers suddenly in an intense, passionate kiss that left her gasping, staring intently at his hard mouth. 'Oh, God, I want to drown in you! To take you to bed at night and sometimes just hold you until dawn...'

'And other times?' she whispered shakily, her hands thrusting into his thick black hair.

'To ruin you with my body!' he said thickly, eyes darkening.

'Yes...!' she whispered, heart thudding faster. 'Oh, yes!'

He kissed her again, passionately, and then raised his head, breathing harshly. 'You'll marry me?'

'Conor' she said hoarsely, 'I'd marry you six times over if I had to! Sixty times over until the end of time if anyone or anything ever tore us apart again!'

'To hell and back?' he asked, eyes blazing.

'Yes...to hell and back!'

'So where does that leave us now?' he asked, staring at her mouth.

'Darling...under a blood-red sky!'

Mills & Boon

Next month's Romances

Each month, you can choose from a world of variety in romance with Mills & Boon. These are the new titles to look out for next month.

NO GENTLE SEDUCTION Helen Bianchin

THE FINAL TOUCH Betty Neels

TWIN TORMENT Sally Wentworth

JUNGLE ENCHANTMENT Patricia Wilson

DANCE FOR A STRANGER Susanne McCarthy

THE DARK SIDE OF DESIRE Michelle Reid

WITH STRINGS ATTACHED Vanessa Grant

BARRIER TO LOVE Rosemary Hammond

FAR FROM OVER Valerie Parv

HIJACKED HONEYMOON Eleanor Rees

DREAMS ARE FOR LIVING Natalie Fox

PLAYING BY THE RULES Kathryn Ross

ONCE A CHEAT Jane Donnelly

HEART IN FLAMES Sally Cook

KINGFISHER MORNING Charlotte Lamb

STARSIGN

STING IN THE TAIL Annabel Murray

Available from Boots, Martins, John Menzies, W.H. Smith, Woolworths and other paperback stockists.

Also available from Mills and Boon Reader Service, P.O. Box 236, Thornton Road, Croydon, Surrey CR9 3RU.